ASHES TO ASHES

THE GARDENER

MILTON & HUGO L.L.C.
4407 Park Ave., Suite 5
Union City, NJ 07087, USA

Website: *www. miltonandhugo.com*
Hotline: *1- 888-778-0033*
Email: *info@miltonandhugo.com*

Ordering Information:
Quantity sales. Special discounts are granted to corporations, associations, and other organizations. For more information on these discounts, please reach out to the publisher using the contact information provided above.

Library of Congress Control Number: 2024927056
ISBN-13:   979-8-89285-392-7   [Paperback Edition]
              979-8-89285-393-4   [Hardback Edition]
              979-8-89285-394-1   [Digital Edition]

Rev. date: 05/12/2025

1

Mount Olympus is in shambles as Ares is brandishing his spear and Phobos is holding his trident. Eris is also with them holding her bident. They approach Zeus's chamber.

Athena stands there with Demeter, waiting outside the doors of Zeus's chambers. She hears their footsteps and summons her short sword with a white pearl handle.

Ares's helmet becomes visible as they walk up the steps, and Athena says frantically, "Brother, what is the point of this?"

Ares's full body comes in sight with Eris and Phobos. Ares points his spear at her, responding to her in hostility, "The gods shall no longer interfere with the mortal world."

Athena looks at the weapons Eris and Phobos are holding.She looks shocked and stammers out, "Are those...no, Ares...you animal." Demeter tries to supress her emotions as her voice barely cracks out one sentence "what of my daughter?" Ares sighs as Demeter heart sinks to her stomach as she hears Ares say "she fought well to defend her husband." Demeter falls to ground as she tries to coup with her daughter's death.

Ares continues, "They would not see sense, so they will not see anything now."

Athena shrinks down in a nearby chair next to Demeter out of Ares's way, shocked and in disbelief that her uncles are gone. Demeter gets up and looks at Ares as she says quietly "I will never forgive you Ares, I will go to Taurus for my daughter body". Demeter walks away slowly like a ghost. Ares remembers the warning as he continues on his mission as he walks past his sister quietly saying "Soon you shall see why, sister." He walks in and sees his father armed and primed with the thunderbolt, ready to strike.

Zeus strikes a thunderbolt at Ares. Phobos quickly blocks it with his trident and sends it back through in the form of a powerful water stream. The water hits Zeus, knocking him down as the water splashes around him. He slowly stands back up and throws another strike as Eris uses Hades's bident weapon and releases sulfur fumes, causing him to choke on it, making him miss the bolt. The bolt cracks near a wall, making a thunderous sound. Ares sees where the bolt hit and keeps walking to him. Eris clears the air around Zeus.

Zeus looks up and sees Ares's spear inches away from his throat. Zeus relaxes and tosses the bolt away from him, knowing he is defeated, and he says, "You are not fit for this job, son."

Ares removes his spear from his throat and takes off his helmet and sets it on a table, with the metal prongs making a murderous sound. He says, "I do not crave your job, just a decent father."

Zeus looks at him and laughs as he says, "So this is what this is about. What do you want me to say, I am proud of you?"

Ares gives back a deadly grin, making Zeus shiver, then he says, "No, I am past that, Father. This world deserves better."

Zeus gulps as he says, "What about them? You will not harm my children, Ares."

Ares steps back and takes a seat, saying, "Agreed, even though I do not see the point in your pets. They shall not be harmed. However, no more demigods or direct interference from the divine."

Zeus's eyes look reluctant, but he nods in agreement, as he stands up and says, "I shall shut down the portal to the mortal plane, but what about the ones on earth currently?"

Ares grabs a chair next to him and slides him a chair. Zeus grabs the chair and pulls it to the table as Ares continues, "I will use your bolt and hunt them down."

Zeus shakes his head and says, "Chasing down other half gods with my weapon is wrong."

Ares retorts, "Interfering with mortals is wrong. Disgracing your matrimony is wrong. There is a huge list of things that are wrong while we still tinker with their world."

Zeus cannot find a valid argument against Ares, so he says, "This is going to change everything, Ares."

Ares responds, "I hope so."

Zeus thinks.

As Ares feels his thoughts flowing, he breaks the silence. "What are you thinking about, Father?"

Zeus responds calmly, "I need to rename myself, son. I cannot be Zeus without interfering with humanity."

Ares thinks for a while and says, "You can still be the almighty in different ways." He pauses as he continues, "To the more pressing matter, I will handle the demigods and offer them sanctuary here, if it makes you feel better."

Zeus responds quickly, "If they refuse?"

Ares stays silent as an answer. Zeus sighs, and Ares continues, "The demons on earth need to be addressed."

Zeus responds, "I can handle the demons."

Ares looks at him, confused, as he says, "They are like roaches. They hide, and in great number, it will take millenniums to cleanse."

Zeus smiles as he says, "There is more magic than you know, son."

Ares looks at his father, confused. "What do you mean?"

Zeus sighs deeply. "I will give up a part of my being to rid of them and also to say I love them." Zeus sighs as he continues, "I will need go down two more times, son, to set the standard straight."

Zeus pauses a moment as he continues, "It will be a clean slate, and they will have the right to choose." He looks at Phobos and Ares, then asks, "Are my brothers really dead?"

Ares nods his head as he says, "They all put up a fight. However, they would not give up their claim to your throne. Some of them tried to bargain with me."

Zeus nods his head and says, "They were never going to give up anyways."

Ares respectfully says, "One more thing, Father."

Zeus looks annoyed, but he begrudgingly asks, "What is it, son?"

Ares stands up and holds his hands out for the weapons as his children hand them over. He takes the trident and bident as Zeus stares at him. Ares slams the trident in front of Phobos and says, "He is now the controller of the oceans."

Eris looks at Ares and says, "What about me, Father?"

Ares looks at her and says, "I will not condemn my daughter to the depths of Tartarus. I want you to find a good husband."

Eris looks disgusted as she says, "My reward is being betrothed."

Zeus starts to laugh.

Eris snaps at Zeus, "What do you find humorous, Defeated God?"

Ares pulls her attention back to him and says, "He let us win, daughter. Soon I will give you something formidable, but just give me time." Eris looks at Ares annoyed as she storms out of the room.

Zeus says, "It's not as easy as it looks, son."

Ares retakes his seat and says, "I never expect easy, Father."

Zeus looks at Ares and says, "On that note, son, I am proud of you. I shall honor your relationship with Aphrodite."

Ares looks at him, confused, as he says, "What changed your mind?"

Zeus stands up and says, "You took down Titans just to do what is right by your heart. That's all I could ever ask for."

Ares looks at him even more confused.

Athena storms, ready for battle as she sees them talking.

Zeus looks at his favorite daughter as he says, "Me and your brother are talking, not fighting."

Athena sighs as she says, "Thank the stars."

Zeus looks at his bolt. "I no longer have need of this anymore, daughter. When your brother is done with my weapon, I shall infuse you with it."

Athena stays silent, unsure what has even happened. She looks at her brother, unsure, then says, "What happened?"

Ares looks at his sister calmly, then says, "We have negotiated peace, sister. Is that really so hard to believe?"

Athena looks at her brother questioningly. "You are not taking the bolt?"

Ares looks at the bolt, then says, "I know myself, sister, and I know that bolt carries responsibility. I do not want more responsibility."

Athena looks at Ares, confused, and says, "What responsibilities do you have?"

Ares responds quickly, "I have the place that warriors go."

Athena looks at him, annoyed, as she responds, "You bribed the boatman to do that for you."

Ares smiles as he says, "Still my responsibility. Even your owl would agree." He stands up and moves slowly to her and reaches for her brace carefully as he says, "If I ever need the bolt, I know where to find it."

Zeus breathes in and smiles, then says, "I am glad my children are finally getting along."

Ares lets go of her and says to Zeus, "Let's not get ahead of the situation now." He looks at his father and claps his hand as he says, "Well, I had a long day, so I am going to go home, and I am sure you all have a lot of stuff to talk about."

Zeus stands up. "One last thing, son." He pulls a bottle from a shelf and pours three glasses and hands them out. He looks at his children and grandchildren and says a toast. "To a better tomorrow."

Ares slams the drink as they sip, and then Phobos and Ares start to walk away.

Athena looks shocked as she protests, "You should be a part of the planning, brother."

Ares answers while Phobos and he are walking away, "Not my responsibility, sister."

They walk out.

As Zeus and Athena sit, they hear a baby crying out. Zeus gets up and attends to the baby.

Athena stands up and joins him, and she looks at the beautiful baby. "Why is this baby so beautiful?"

Zeus holds the baby as it starts to coo. He responds, "Because he is the morning star."

Athena looks at the baby as she says, "Lucifer?"

Zeus smiles while playing with the baby. "Indeed, my beautiful daughter, the firstborn with the human race in mind."

2

Ares and Athena crash-land on Pompeii in a ball of crimson and thunder that appears to be a meteorite. Athena rolls on the summit as she tries to regain her control. Ares hits the ground feet first and stabs his sword deep in the mountain. As it slams, it makes a deep stone breaking sound. He tries to regain control of his body. A gas begins to leak out of the fissure of the volcano. Athena stands up in her silver and black armor. She stares at Ares as he begins to stand up in his black and gold armor. He takes off his black with gold trim helmet and looks at her. She begins to start up with their armor scrapped and torn up. He draws his dagger on his chest.

She pulls her sword and yells at Ares in a disciplinary tone, "Honestly, brother, this has to be one of most idiotic ideas you have ever had in our existence!"

Ares looks at her in disgust and replies in a stoic voice, "It's only idiotic if you do not see the danger that is about to happen. I get it, my so…righteous sister."

Athena continues to argue. "The Titans have been locked in hell for eons, and you want to go and end them. Even for the angel of war, that is low for you."

Ares begins to get agitated. "On the contrary, I am only preserving the future of this world, and I do not understand why you continue to be a headache of mine, when you should be our father's headache," he responds.

Three more lights fall out of the sky in the middle of the banter.

Aphrodite lands close to Ares.

He looks back and sees her in her rose-gold breastplate, ready to back Ares if need be. He looks at her and says in a loving voice, "How are you, my love?"

Aphrodite smiles at Ares and responds, "Just making sure you quit making friends everywhere you go."

Euphrosyne and Demeter land next to Athena, ready for war.

Euphrosyne yells at Ares, "Will you please use reason for once in your life, you brute?"

Ares yells back, "Yeah, when you start using your spine alone instead of relying on everyone else to hold your weight, you runt of the litter!" His angelic form begins to show as his face starts to turn into a form of a jackal.

Euphrosyne looks at Athena, and she states, "Do not look to me to fight your battles."

Ares sees an opportunity and goes for his sword. It is still in the mountain.

Athena yells as Ares grabs it, "You will kill them all!"

It is too late. Ares has already pulled the sword out, and the volcano begins to erupt.

Another bright light shines over where the sword is stopping the vapor.

Saint Michael walks out of the light and says, "What is the meaning of this volcano going off before it is supposed to?"

Ares responds, "Well, look at that. It is God's hall monitor that I call a brother."

Michael quickly looks over to Ares and says, "Why is it always you that needs to be bailed out?"

Athena giggles and mutters, "I can contest that."

Ares says in a snappy tone, "Of course, you would, because you have numbers, you coward."

Michael, getting more annoyed, shouts, "Enough, everyone. Why is this volcano going off right now!"

Athena chimes in, "Because Ares wants to kill the Titans."

Michael looks at Ares and says in a defeated voice, "Is this true?"

Aphrodite speaks up. "It actually makes a lot of sense."

Michael looks at Aphrodite and says, "If only you were as smart as you are beautiful."

Ares's eyes light up, and he draws his shield. He takes a couple of steps toward Michael.

"What did you say, babysitter?"

Aphrodite, not liking the comment, can sense Ares is about to go to war for a sentence, so she pulls Ares back. He puts up some difficulty but eventually gives in and falls back.

Athena tells him, "Look, we can talk about this later. Maybe even come to a comprise, but just not today. What do you say, Ares?"

Ares looks at Aphrodite and can see her pleading with her eyes. Annoyed, he responds, "Fine." He puts away his weapons, and the group follows suit.

Euphrosyne, Athena, and Demeter summon their wings and go back to heaven.

Aphrodite whispers in Ares's ear, "Please, let's return home, my husband."

Ares nods in agreement and summons his wings, a crimson red with gold tips. She summons hers as well, a dark red that fades in to pink tips.

Michael looks at them and commands, "Ares, please linger a moment with me, brother."

Ares looks at Aphrodite, and she says quietly, "Please do not be long, my love, and try to be civilized."

Ares looks at her in a playful tone. "I am always civilized, love."

She shakes her head and then heads to heaven.

Ares calmly walks over to Michael, who is now looking over the town. He says in a tired tone, "Almost all of these will die now because of your actions here today. Do you know who was down there?"

Ares responds, "Everyone has to die eventually, even us, brother."

Michael shakes his and says in a low voice, "Not everything has to die on your time, Ares."

Ares states back, "True, but everyone has a price to pay, and I can see the evil in this city as well as the good. I'll let God sort them out."

Michael tries to explain. "I don't think you get it. There were philosophers and doctors. The young that could have changed the world for the better, brother. Now none of that will come to light."

Ares sits there and listens to Michael's monologue as he knows he can be long-winded.

Michael continues, "Peter says that one day you will have to walk the earth again, and I cannot for the life me understand why when your actions are so reckless."

Ares speaks to defend himself. "I'm sure when I walk the earth again, it will be the death of you, brother. On the other hand, let me ask you this—we were both designed for war, brother, but what makes you think that you are better than me?"

Michael snaps back, "Even if we could go back to our very existence, I still would not have enough time to tell you why."

Ares laughs and says, "I can tell you in one sentence why all of your time you need to describe why you think you are better—you really are *not*."

Intrigued, Michael looks at him, waiting for an answer.

Ares smiles and says, "I don't deny my design, and my design is war. There is honor in my wars and warriors. I accept the truth. And the truth is blood, sweat, and tear. I call it my holy trinity." Ares looks at the city and mutters, "They are really all dead?"

Michael responds, "Unfortunately, yes, brother."

Ares shakes his head and calmly says, "Shame."

Michael, getting more irritated by his lack of compassion, commands Ares, "Go home to your wife, Ares. I do not know what she sees in you."

Ares smiles and looks at him. "She lost a bet." He laughs and takes off to heaven.

Ares arrives back to heaven and walks into his house and sees Aphrodite in a white toga with her right arm covered and the left uncovered. Ares stares at her and moves closer to her. When he gets closer, he hears Athena's voice. Ares tries to slink away, but he is quickly stopped by Aphrodite's voice.

"Where do you think you are going, husband?"

Ares moves closer and looks at Athena, then back at Aphrodite.

He sighs and says, "I was hoping this was just girl talk." He turns to them, seeing none of them are amused. He turns to Athena and sees her sitting at their table wearing a silver dress with long sleeves. She looks up and sees Ares wearing his tight black shirt with his right sleeve missing. He looks at Athena, then at Aphrodite.

With attitude, she turns to him and says, "She came out of goodwill, my love."

Ares quietly says, "She always does supposedly."

Athena stands up and states, "You know I am right here."

Ares looks at her and calmly says as he takes a seat, "How could I not know, sister?"

Athena quickly says, "I come to broker peace, brother. Please let me say my piece."

Ares hand signals to her, and Aphrodite smacks the back of his head. He looks back at her, and she stares at him and says, "She deserves a response. She is your sister."

Ares grunts and hand signals to Athena.

Athena impatiently says, "It's okay, Aphrodite. I know my brother and his stubbornness, so I'll just say my piece and be done." She turns to Ares and begins her statement. "Brother, I can almost agree with you, but where I draw the line is killing a caged animal. It is cruel and immoral."

Ares snaps at her aggressively, "Sister, do not preach me to about morals. I believe you're starting to see yourself as the Greeks see you."

Athena responds, "Be that as it may, it is still cruel."

Ares presses the argument. "If the Titans had their way, we would be shackled and chained, if not executed, and I can appreciate the execution more than be a caged animal. So, my dear sister, I see it as a mercy. No one should be forced to live in a small room being tortured by their mind and demons. I believe it is you who is immoral."

Athena sits and thinks on his word. As much as she does not want to agree with him, he has brought up a good point. They sit for a while, and she finally speaks up.

"Either way, brother, press the humanity one more time, and by the rules that you have set, you will be in hell with the Titans. Mom or me won't be able to save you, brother. Please take heed of my words."

Ares looks at her with control of the situation. He responds carefully, "Sister, I stopped needing someone to come and save me when Father disowned me and everyone shunned and shamed me for being who I am. Athena, I know the truth—no one is coming to save me, nor do I truly need them to save me." He starts to feel a burning stare from Aphrodite. He turns to her, and Athena can sense she is about to be stuck in their argument.

She says quickly, "I have said my piece. I shall take my leave." She stands and quickly leaves.

Aphrodite is staring at Ares's head as he tries to quickly say but is cut off by her.

"So no one is coming to save you, hmm…"

He says sheepishly, "You know what I meant."

She walks to the window and starts watching the world. He leans against the wall and tries to pull her.

She slaps his hand away and angrily says, "Even if you were dead, I would find a way to be with you."

Ares smiles at her.

She sees him smiling and snaps at him, "I am not joking, Ares!"

Ares looks at her and says calmly, "I am sorry. I can be over exaggerated sometimes."

She turns back and says, "Finally, you admit that you are not perfect."

Ares is still staring at her.

She turns around and looks at Ares, and she mutters, "Why are you always staring at me?"

Ares responds, "I can't believe you are here with me."

Aphrodite smiles and makes her way to the loft. She lies down and playfully says, "You know females respond to confidence."

Ares makes his way to her and kisses her lightly. "What about overconfidence?"

Aphrodite laughs and kisses him again. "Equally a turnoff."

Ares looks at her, confused. "So what is wrong with you?"

She looks at him with playful shock.

Ares smiles at her and makes his way to look out the window. "What's going on with Earth anyways? What were you watching?"

Aphrodite joins Ares at the window as he says, "The holy war is going on. I have blessed some soldiers. I am currently waiting for them to almost have victory, then pulls my support. Plus, they are working on something very dark. They have sparked my interest. I want to see how they are doing it."

Aphrodite grabs a plate of ambrosia. Ares sees the plate and takes a couple of pieces. He returns to the couch where Aphrodite is sprawled out. He taps her legs, and she does not move them. He puts the plate down and picks her up.

She says, laughing, "That's not fair."

Ares smiles and puts her on top of him and says while he strokes her hair, "What is it you told me a long time ago? All is fair in love and war."

Aphrodite says, "You mean when I fell in love with you."

He responds, "I know you always wanted me since the first day we met."

Aphrodite quickly responds, "If I remember correctly, it was you who said I would give you the world."

Ares looks annoyed and retorts, "And you said the world is not yours to give." He continues, "However, I do not recall specifying which world."

Aphrodite flirtingly says, "Oh, which world did you give me?"

Ares holds her closely and whispers, "Mine to combine with yours, love and war, patience and haste." He can hear the window and senses humanity is about to do something irrational. He squeezes Aphrodite and asks her to get some wine.

She smiles and says, "Of course."

He walks to the window and looks down and can see the pope and the Lion heart about to lose the holy war.

Aphrodite speaks from down the hall. "Anything interesting happening?"

Ares says sternly, "Desperation," Aphrodite comes jogging with one glass and a bottle. She reaches Ares and looks at Earth through the window. Ares reaches for the glass, and she pours a drink for him. He raises it to toast her, and she taps the bottle against his glass. He looks at her and smiles.

Aphrodite says in a loving tone, "I know how you get when you have too much, and we don't need interfering in anymore earthly manners, just enough to keep you alive and healthy, my love."

Ares just smiles and continues to watch. He watches intently and looks around.

Aphrodite can feel him scanning around and sighs and says, "What are you looking for, the children you call Spartans? Or maybe the whore nest that you call the Amazons?"

He looks at her and says in a questioning tone, "You really hated the warrior women?"

Aphrodite responds sharply, "They have not given proper tribute, and the fact their loyalty changed so quickly is what bugs me. How dare they compare themselves to me?"

Ares laughs and comments, "That was enough for you and my sister to send them to their death with Hercules?"

Aphrodite moves in closer and hugs Ares from behind, resting her head on his back. He takes her hands and leads her to stand in front of him.

Aphrodite raises her head up and says, "Plus they wanted you, and you are mine."

Ares just smiles and kisses her forehead. Ares calmly says, "I was looking at the wars going on. A lot of prayers are being said to me. I was just seeing what they are up to and against."

Aphrodite looks back down at the world, and she says, "Anything of note?"

Ares says quietly, "Nothing of note so far. Everyone that is praying to me has been under control. If they don't, they will join my hall of warriors to join in drink, food, and battle."

Aphrodite sighs and says, "Your little game room."

Ares pulls her closely and whispers, "My second paradise compared to being with you, my love. However, look what is going on in the holy war."

—⚋—

The holy war starts to shift as the Muslims begin to turn the tide of war. The pope and the grand master look over the battlefield with frustration. The grand master shouts commands at his generals to push through, but the defeat is evident on their faces.

The pope looks to his cardinals and quietly says, "Is there anything we can do to save this battle and war?"

The cardinals look at each other, not sure what to say.

Finally, one speaks up and says, "We have been working on something, but it is not ready yet. We are still working out the energy source and the nature of the ritual."

The pope and the grandmaster look at him with disgust.

The grand master speaks in a commanding tone. "Rituals? As in blasphemy?"

The cardinal replies, "Grand Master, with all due respect, it is our jobs to look into all rituals to make sure it is in the safe hands of the church. Rather us than them, right?"

The grand master looks at the pope with a disapproving look and asks, "Is it true? You gave them the role to look into heresy of nature."

The pope responds confidently, "There are many things that the Templars would disapprove of, but it is my duty as the envoy of God to look and seize such power for the church to seal away."

The grand master continues to protest. "We win by the grace of God, so fight for the grace of God."

The pope says in a commanding voice, "I am the voice of God."

The cardinal who spoke before speaks up again. "Perhaps if you can see it, you would change your mind, Grand Master."

The pope stares at him, his expression filled with betrayal.

The grand master sees the look on his face and says, "It is here in Acre? I thought we were here for the grail?"

The pope says, "That was the reason, but we have found a script that they have been working on that appears to be the work of angels."

The grand master says calmly, "Finally, God bestows a favor on the battle."

The pope responds, "Or a curse."

The grand master looks at him in confusion. He recognizes the stare and says calmly, "Let me show me you, my son."

The pope and the cardinals turn around and start walking. The grand master takes one more and can see his men getting slaughtered but still fighting valiantly. He thinks, *If I could save lives that fight for*

God and his will, I shall embrace all I need to. He turns and walks with the pope.

The pope and his cardinals, followed by the grand master, reach a cave that has been sealed; and only one door that has been built for maximum security stands to be tried.

The pope walks up and says, "Vivant Deus."

Two guards come out of holes from the side and begin to unlock the gate, then the door. The pope turns and makes the sign of the cross, blessing them who are following him.

The grand master nods but still looks unsure about this pope.

Seeing his concerned look, the pope says, "Patience, my son, you will see everything."

It does not comfort him at all.

The door has finally been unlocked, and they light a torch and begin to walk inside. The moment the grandmaster gets in, he immediately gets cold shivers, as if he just felt the cold of a winter breeze hit him.

As they continue down, he can see something watching him but cannot find who it is. They begin to hear chanting followed by candlelight. The grand master sees a shadowy figure on the wall, its hand shaped like a claw and pointing downward. It vanishes as they turn the corner.

The grand master looks at the people there and sees five witches with open books and dead animals. He covers his nose and says, "The stench of this place."

The pope responds quietly, "They require a lot of animals."

The grand master looks and finally snaps, "God will judge you for actions of blasphemy and being a heretic."

The pope says in a stoic tone, "Save your judgment till you see it."

A witch finally approaches them and says in a hissing tone, "You have interrupted our channeling. Why?"

The pope says in commanding tone, "We are here to check and see a demonstration of your findings."

The witch looks at the grand master and begins examining him with her eyes and speaks slowly. "He has a very pure energy, barely tarnished by time. Perhaps we could use him."

The pope responds quickly, "We are just here to see the progress, not to help."

The witch walks away to a table with a drawing carved into the wood and says quietly, "I was not asking. If you want this to work, we need pure humans."

The grand master speaks up. "I do not wish to be a part of heretic ways."

The witch laughs and says in her hissing tone, "You claim us to be heretics, but from we stand, we know more about your god than your book. Tell me, Grand Master, have you seen an angel?"

The grand master stays silent.

The witch continues, "Thought as much. We have been communicating with one that has brought us this far. Please come and observe and be my audience." She points to a place on the ground, not taking her eyes off the table, looking over markings.

Ares and Aphrodite are watching.

Ares whispers to the grand master, "See where this goes, faithful soldier."

The grand master looks around to see where the voice was coming from.

The pope notices and proceeds to ask him, "What is wrong, my child?"

The grand master refocuses on the situation at hand and responds, "Nothing, Your Holiness. This cave seems to have lots of secrets."

The pope nods.

The witch notices the change in energy as well and looks around.

The pope begins to get an eerie feeling while replying, "I was caught quite off guard when they found something as well."

They move to the part of the ground and see lines that form a pentagram.

The grand master asks, "What is the meaning of this?"

The witch takes her eyes off the table and moves to him and signals to her other witches to bring in prisoners. Four unfortunate souls, shackled and nearly clinging to life, walk and are placed over the points of the pentagram.

The witch looks at the grand master and says to him, "What would you do to save this war and the men who fight in it?"

The grand master looks at her and says in a growl, "Leave them out of this."

The witch responds quickly, "I am trying to save them, but my soul is tarnished and unusable. However, you have a soul that is untarnished and pure. If you make a sacrifice of your blood, sweat, and tears, you could have the power to win this war, Grand Master."

The grand master looks at the pope and angrily shouts, "Is this what we have resorted to, witchcraft and sacrifices!"

The pope responds in an argumentative tone, "Our soldiers are the sacrifice already. We have lost how many souls and people to this war."

The grand master looks at the pope in disgust.

The witch chimes in again, "What say you, Grand Master? Will you save your men?"

The grand master pauses and thinks and remembers seeing his men getting slaughtered and begrudgingly agrees with a nod.

Ares looks at Aphrodite in confusion but is proud of his conviction.

Aphrodite says in a confused manner, "Is he one of your men?"

Ares responds, "I have no idea who this man is."

The grand master begins to take off his armor till only his monk dress is left. He takes his place at the top of the pentagram. He looks at the witch and says, "What awaits?"

The witch says calmly, "Pain. We need everyone here to bleed." She signals to the witches with her hands, and they come out with whips with metal tips. She continues, "This will hurt, but I need you to think of the men and everything you hold dear." She looks at the other witches and nods to cut the throat of the prisoners and hold them over the lines. The blood leads to the center of the pentagram. The witch walks over to the grand master and says quietly, "Are you ready to begin?"

The grand master looks at the pope and says, "If I die, tell my men I did what I could. I shall meet them at the gates as a commander should."

The pope nods to the cardinal, and the cardinal writes it down.

The grand master looks at the witch and says in a hateful tone, "May God have mercy on your soul."

She smiles, showing her black teeth, and she begins.

He takes the first few with a straight face, but as she continues, he begins to bleed. Eventually, he falls to pain.

Ares, looking down gently, tells the grand master, "Blood, sweat, and tears, my child. You have paid the entry fee for you and your soldiers. They shall meet you again, my fellow warrior."

Aphrodite looks at Ares and comments, "Should you have done that?"

Ares just shrugs his shoulders and retorts with, "Someone needs to have mercy and let him go. This was not in vain." He looks at her and finishes with, "Whatever it is they are doing."

The grand master starts screaming. As the blood begins to almost make it to the center, he yells, "Forgive me, my father!"

The blood reaches the middle and ignites, and everyone who has donated is turned to ash. The ashes make their way to the middle and begins to form an ember mold. As the ashes fall away, a mask is revealed. The group cautiously walks over to examine the mask. It is flat black with a golden helmet on one cheek and a sword on the other, with crimson lenses covering the eyes.

The pope looks at the witches and says, "The deal has been done. You are free to live on the outskirts of France. You are not to be persecuted." He looks at the cardinal and holds his hand out. The cardinal hands him a scroll, and the pope hands it to the witch. The pope turns to the cardinal and says in a domineering voice, "Lock this in the Vatican. What has happened here right now has never happened."

The cardinals nod, and the witches begin to leave. One of them turns around and says in her hissing voice, "I'll see you in our holy land, Father."

Ares, standing there dumbfounded, finally manages to look at Aphrodite and sternly remarks, "That was a hell of a show."

Aphrodite, looking scared, quietly asks Ares, "Did you have anything to do with this?"

Ares, shocked at her question, quickly responds, "I have no hand in this."

Aphrodite points to the mask and asks, "Then why is the engraving yours?"

Ares takes a second look and stares at the helmet and sword. He looks at her and says, "I can assure you I had no play in this."

They hear banging at their door, and they turn to face it.

They hear a voice call out, "Ares!"

Aphrodite looks at Ares and says to him quietly, "Athena."

Ares stands up straight and walks to the door. Before he could open the door, it is kicked in, knocking Ares back. Michael and Athena rush in, followed by Erichthonius. Ares quickly gets up and summons his armor and prepares for an all-out war. Athena stops and slams her spear in the floor, which crackles with electricity.

Ares growls, "What is the meaning of this, you plebes?"

Michael walks up and states, "You have violated your own rules by interfering with humanity firsthand."

Ares stands up and questions, "No one saw us on Pompeii, you imbecile."

Athena looks at him and sternly responds, "We are not talking about that incident. We are talking about the humans making your mask on earth."

Ares gets back in a defensive stance.

Aphrodite gets behind Ares and shouts, "He had nothing to do with that! We are just as confused as you!"

Athena looks like she isn't buying it and yells, "Ares, you are to be shackled and taken to Hermes!"

Ares responds quietly but in a joking manner, "Only Aphrodite can bind me, and what we do is none of your concern, dear sister."

Athena aggressively responds, "This isn't a joke, brother."

Aphrodite whispers to him, "Just go. You know you are innocent of these crimes."

Ares lowers his guard and responds, "I'll go willingly, but you are not putting me in shackles."

Athena looks at Michael, and Michael nods in agreement. They begin to walk out of their house, and Aphrodite comes up behind Ares and hugs and kisses him before he goes.

Ares looks down and sets his eyes on Erichthonius. He smiles and jokingly says, "How are you doing, Tail?"

Erichthonius looks around and sees he is talking about his tail. He looks at Ares. Feeling offended, he turns and whips Ares with his scale tail, breaking the skin above his eyes. Athena looks at what just happened to Ares. She walks over to him and picks up his shaved head and begins to examine him over. Then she drops his head, and he looks up. His gold blood starts to run into his eye.

She states, "He will survive, but he shall make it there with no more injuries. Are we understood? He is still my brother." Athena looks at Erichthonius.

He looks down and quietly says, "Yes, Mother."

Ares shakes the blood off and continues to ridicule Erichthonius. "One of these days I will cut your tail off and whip you with it, you abomination."

Athena turns around and faces Ares and says in a stern voice, "You will not harm my son, and like it or hate it, he is your nephew, Ares."

Ares responds, "I am just testing you, sister. Plus I just wanted to see if he is a fighter or a thinker."

Athena retorts, "He just almost made you half blind."

Ares smiles and says, "Just like his mother, just enough to try to scare you but never enough to finish the job."

—⁂—

Athena looks up and sees Saint Peter, also known as Hermes. Athena says quietly under her breath with relief, "Finally, we are here."

They see Saint Peter reading a book, flipping through pages in a slow and dramatic manner.

Ares steps up to Saint Peter and states, "Hermes, for the love of my father, you must see that I have been framed." He is joking, but in a serious tone, he says, "My coins are on the tail whipper over there."

Saint Peter does not move his eyes or his focus from his book.

Ares continues to protest and seems to throw a tantrum. He says in a growl, "This was a pact I made. Why would I break the own truce I made with my father?"

Saint Peter finally raises his hand for silence.

Ares looks at him with confusion.

Saint Peter slowly and sternly starts to say, "First things first, Ares, I am now Saint Peter, the guardian of the heavenly gates. Secondly, I do not believe you to be the type to break a law that you made. However, right now, from what I can gather, it was your energy present at the scene."

Ares quickly defends himself, "I gave the sacrifices, my blessing for Valhalla."

Saint Peter responds, "They are no longer your sacrifices, Ares. Why did you give your blessings after?"

Ares says confusingly, "I can give my blessing after. It kind of defeats the purpose of it."

Saint Peter flips to another page and says quietly, "What is the purpose of your blessing, Ares?"

Ares says in a proud tone, "To give comfort to the warriors who think they have been abandoned, so they now at least have some angels to care about them."

Saint Peter retorts with another question, "Do you think that your father cares for them? After all, this war is in his honor. They believe this war is going to bring them closer to him. So I ask again, Ares, do you believe that they don't feel loved by the father?"

Ares looks down, not wanting to answer to the question. He stays silent.

Athena, getting impatient, states in an aggressive manner, "He asked a question, Ares."

Ares snarls with his angelic jackal face.

Saint Peter slams the book shut, making a boom that breaks the attention of the battle. Saint Peter calmly says, "Ares, you are to remain in your house and not to come out until I can figure out what has happened."

Ares cheerfully states, "I can agree to that—a vacation with me and Aphrodite."

Saint Peter quickly interrupts Ares, saying, "Without Aphrodite. She shall live in God's palace till this is resolved."

Ares looks even more annoyed and angered than before. He looks at Saint Peter and says in relaxed tone, "This is not justice. This is belittling and shaming. You have already judged me for being guilty, have you not, Hermes?"

Saint Peter tries to say in a sympathetic tone, "It is to make sure—"

He is quickly interrupted by Ares. "To make sure I'm not happy."

Saint Peter doesn't look up.

Ares growls, "This will lead to a war, Hermes, and you know it."

Saint Peter waves his hands, and bonds materialize around Ares's wrists, pulling them together. Ares tries to break the crimson cuffs that are flaring from his wrist but to no avail. The clamps are fully arresting him.

Saint Peter throws a rope to Athena and calmly says, "Athena the Righteous, will you please escort Ares the Warlord back to his room?"

Saint Michael looks at Ares. As they are moving him, he says to him "You did this to yourself, brother. Don't worry, I'll take care of Aphrodite for you."

Ares snarls and tries to bite Saint Michael but is met by Athena's fist, knocking him out.

Ares wakes up on the floor of his house. He looks up and begins to get up, calling out, "Wife." There is no answer. He begins to move around, holding on the walls, as he searches the house. "Aphrodite." He walks to the window and sees a black figure standing outside. His vision is still blurry, so he rubs his eyes and sees the figure more clearly—the devil in a black robe.

The figure turns around and shows his beautiful face as the devil says, "How are you, brother?"

Ares mutters, "How hard did Athena hit me?"

The devil replies, "Quite hard. I heard the thunder all the down in the depths of hell."

Ares takes a seat on his couch and says, "What do you want, Lucifer?"

Lucifer responds, "The question is what do you want, Ares?"

Ares says confidently, "Nothing that you can guarantee."

Lucifer laughs and says, "I always liked you, brother."

Ares says in a proud voice, "I have something I need to get done, so if you could make your point so we could be done with this, that would be fantastic."

Lucifer takes a seat next to Ares and pulls out his hand. A glass ball appears in his hand, and he says, "Take a glance."

Ares says, "I do not have time for these games."

Lucifer moves the ball in a suggestive manner. Ares looks at Lucifer, and Lucifer is staring in the ball. Ares finally gives in and sees Aphrodite crying on Saint Michael's shoulder.

Ares says unsurely, "She would not dare. There is no way."

Lucifer says in a calm manner, "I can give you guys a way out and get you guys as close as I can to each other."

Ares, still staring at the ball, says, "In return for what?"

Lucifer closes his hand into a fist and says, "My demons are becoming unruly. I need someone to rule the violent circle of hell. In other words, do what you do best, Ares, and I can get you your wife in hell with you."

Ares begins to think and says, "You can get her into hell. Do you understand?"

Lucifer smiles. "Of course, brother." Lucifer holds his hand out for a handshake. Ares can only see Aphrodite crying on Saint Michael. He takes his hand, and a dark circle begins to form around them. His veins start to turn dark as if poison was running through him. Lucifer grins, showing his black teeth. Ares falls to the ground. His wings come out, and his feathers start to fall out. Ares groans in pain. He looks up to Lucifer. His eyes are a golden amber now, and they look like they are filled with hatred. Then Ares vanishes into hell through a black pentagram on the floor. Lucifer looks at the ground and sees the burnt sulfur stains on the floor.

—⚏—

Athena is making her rounds and decides to stop by to check on Ares as she has a feeling that he is in distress. She makes her way to the door and knocks. She waits for a while, then knocks again, then shouts at the door, "Brother! I have come to offer guidance, maybe even an ear.

I know I am probably one of the few that you do not wish to see right at this moment, but I am here with good intentions."

She knocks again, and the door creeps open. She looks at it and begins to get concerned. She walks in cautiously, unsure if this is a trap or if he has just finally given up. She finally makes her way to the window and sees the pentagram on the floor. She gasps. She begins to move quickly out of the house to raise the alarm, and as she is making her way to the door, she sees the dark figure looking out the door. She immediately summons her sword.

Lucifer giggles and looks at her, taking off his hood, and says, "Calm down. I just wanted to take in the heavenly sights."

Athena holds the sword to his direction and says, "What are you doing here, Lucifer?"

Lucifer points to himself and starts to walk around and says, "I came for the same reason you did, out of love for Ares. You know at one point I considered him a brother too."

Athena responds in an aggressive tone, "You didn't see him as a brother—you saw him as tool."

Lucifer responds with a question, "Let me guess—you see him as a brother or a criminal?"

Athena says back in return, "I see him as my brother regardless of his actions."

Lucifer smiles, showing his black teeth, and says, "Then why did you lock him up?"

Athena looks at him in disgust.

Lucifer continues, "I am not here to judge or argue with you. I am here to try to help our brother."

Athena remains skeptical, still holding her sword, circling him.

Lucifer just stands still and puts his hands up.

Athena regains her train of thought and says, "Where is he?"

Lucifer begins to appear to relax and says, "He made me send him to hell."

Athena immediately gets frustrated and yells at Lucifer, "I swear every time he does something idiotic. Bring him back now!"

Lucifer looks at her with an uncertain face and says, "I cannot do that. He has made a deal with me, and he must stay or suffer God's wrath."

Athena, defeated, says, "What was the deal, Lucifer, you snake?"

Lucifer looks at her, shocked, and says, "You brother pretty much made me. You know how he could be, Athena. He made a thousand-year deal."

Athena looks at him, disgusted. "How could you damn him?"

Lucifer responds sympathetically, "He damned himself, Athena, like he got himself to face judgment."

Athena puts her sword back and takes a seat to look at the pentagram. Lucifer takes a seat with her and is immediately met with a blade to his throat. He slowly stands back up.

Lucifer says, "There is a way to help him."

Athena says begrudgingly, "What do you mean, Lucifer?"

He looks at her and says, "Take part of a deal?"

Athena says, laughing, "This is your idea of helping him, by getting other angels to fall with him."

Lucifer says calmly, "I am just offering an option. Other than that, there is nothing I can do."

Athena sits and thinks about it, and then finally she gives in and says, "How much longer must I be my brother's keeper?"

Lucifer laughs and says, "We are all bound by blood. We just see things differently."

Athena stands up and offers her hand to Lucifer and says, "I will serve half of his sentence."

Lucifer takes her hand and squeezes it, and she falls to the floor, and the same black ink begins to go through her veins as it did Ares. She looks up at Lucifer, and her eyes begin to appear a lightning blue, then she vanishes, just leaving Lucifer in the house. He hears someone approaching. He pulls out his ball and can see it is Saint Michael. He puts his ball away and vanishes into a dark trail on the ground.

Lucifer makes his way to the house, slithering his way under the door till he comes across Aphrodite crying in a single throne. He slithers behind her and shifts back into his true form.

Aphrodite feels a dark presence, and she gets up and looks behind her and sees Lucifer. She says in a shaky voice, "Lucifer, what are you doing here?"

Lucifer says in a stoic tone, "I came to apologize, Aphrodite."

She looks at him and again shakily asks, "What do you mean?"

Lucifer looks down and says, "He called for me and forced me to make a deal with him."

Aphrodite holds her chest and falls down and starts sobbing again. Lucifer makes his way toward her, and she lets off a small blaze around her, pushing Lucifer back. Lucifer gets up and looks at her, who is unable to control her emotions.

He quickly says, "I might have a way to help you though."

Aphrodite looks at him with a fierce fire in her eyes and says in a deep tone, "How?"

Lucifer gulps and says, "Join him in my realm. I know it is not heaven, but it will be yours to control."

Aphrodite asks, "Will he be there?"

Lucifer looks at her eyes and says, "Not at first, but it will happen."

Aphrodite gets up and says, "It is best if I stay here and wait for him."

Lucifer puts a finger to interject, and he says, "I thought of that too, but there is a flip side to that card." Aphrodite looks at him with interest, and he continues, "Heaven still follows some old rules, and someone will come for your hand."

Aphrodite quickly responds, "I shall refuse any other suitors."

Lucifer says quietly, "They are already making a competition for your hand, and there are some unlikely fellows that are already preparing, one of them you have already explored the option."

She looks at him and says shakily, "Hephaestus?"

Lucifer nods and says, "He is planning your death as his wife to get back at Ares."

Aphrodite begins sobbing again.

He continues, "And Saint Michael."

Aphrodite says through her tears, "He was just in here trying to be a friend."

Lucifer looks at her and says, "That's what you honestly believe, or maybe he's just trying to be your knight in shining armor. They could have given him a chance to defend himself, but they would rather he be gone because it would be easier for them to claim his prizes, glory, and most important to him, his wife."

Aphrodite says, scared, "I need to leave here and be with him."

Lucifer holds out his hand and says, "I'll get you as close to him as I can."

Aphrodite looks at his hand and takes it. The black ink starts to go through her veins, and her eyes start to turn a dark fire red. Her wings start to defeather. She yells in pain. As she is yelling, he smiles, and she is gone through the black pentagram on the floor. He looks around and sees Saint Michael walking to the house to alert Aphrodite of the news. He sees Lucifer and summons his sword.

Lucifer smiles and says, "Soon you will have your war, and you will die."

Saint Michael dashes toward him, and Lucifer falls into the ground, returning back to hell.

Ares looks around his new home. He sees nothing but a vast desert and one house. He walks up to the house and can hear metal scraping. He opens the door and sees a beast with a bullhead and the body of a well-toned man.

The beast growls, "Who enters the domain of Argus?"

Ares laughs and says, "Who names themself Argus?"

Argus turns around and sees a man standing in his door and says, "Who let you out of your circle, mortal?"

Ares looks at him, finding his weaknesses and strengths. Argus sees Ares eyeing him up, and he says, "Don't try it, mortal, and this will save us some time." He turns and goes back to his work.

Ares steps closer and tries to summon his armor and weapons. Nothing happens. He looks confused. Argus fully turns around now, giving Ares his full attention, and says, "I gave you a chance." Argus pulls a machete of the table still covered in blood. He holds it down, with blood draining off it, and begins to step toward Ares. The beast swings the sword in a slashing movement. Ares dodges it and takes a couple of steps back. Argus slowly recovers and looks at Ares. Argus says, "Hold still and let's be done with this."

Ares responds, "You are right, let us be done with this. I am just going to inform you that this is all mine now, including you."

Argus looks at him, shocked; and in a rage, he charges at Ares with his head forward. Ares smiles and catches his horns and throws Argus headfirst in the ground. Argus grunts and gets up, confused. Ares leads the next assault and begins to walk over to his foe, and Argus swings his sword down. Ares dodges it, and the sword hits the ground. Ares stomps on his elbow with a crimson burst, breaking Argus's elbow. Argus gasps in pain, and Ares rips the machete away and examines its craftsmanship and says, "This is a horrible weapon, but it will have to do for right now."

Argus looks at Ares and states, "You are not from the mortal plane. Who are you?"

Ares picks up his head and looks Argus in the eye, and Argus begins to see the crimson swirling in Ares's eyes. Ares puts the machete next to his throat and was about to speak, but then he hears the door open and sees Lucifer walk in.

Lucifer takes one look and says, "See you guys are already acquainted. Argus, I would like you to meet Ares."

Argus looks at Lucifer, confused, and says, "What is the meaning of this, Lucifer? I thought I was the ruler of this realm."

Lucifer smiles and says, "Was. It is now your turn to rest till I am in need of your services later." Lucifer turns his attention to Ares and says, "If you would be so kind to let go of my beast."

Ares does not let go of his focus on Argus and says, "As long as this filth knows his place."

Argus nods, and Ares lets go. Argus rolls over and gets up, then puts himself behind Lucifer, cradling his arm.

Lucifer then says, "This is now yours, Ares, this realm, and where is the houseboy?"

Argus grunts, and a little mouselike creature comes out and makes himself known.

The creature comes out and squeaks, "Yes."

Lucifer looks at the mouse and says, "This is an imp. He is yours to command, Ares."

Ares looks at the imp and says, "Where is she?"

Lucifer says in a consoling voice, "I told you it will take time, Ares."

Ares growls, "I am no longer Ares. I am the realm. I am Violence till she is returned to me."

Lucifer nods, and then they take their leave.

The imp looks at Violence and squeaks, "What is required of me?"

Violence looks at the imp and says, "Do you know how to smith?"

The imp squeaks, "No."

Violence says back quickly, "Then I shall teach you. Come now, we have work to do."

The imp follows.

—⟋⟍—

Lucifer arrives at the circle of hell. It is a gloomy mountain terrain. He begins to walk to where his demon resides. He starts to get close and can hear her talking to someone confused. He hastens his pace. As he walks in, he sees her talking with the imp, making friends with it.

She looks at him and gives him her full attention.

Lucifer looks around, confused.

Aphrodite sees the confusion and says, "It is in the back room."

Lucifer calls out to it, "Aeshma."

Aphrodite looks at him and says in a calm voice, "She is going to need some help getting to you."

Lucifer sighs and walks in the back room. He sees a spear going through Aeshma's donkey head all the way through its eagle body into the ground. The body twitches, signaling it is still clinging to life. Lucifer pulls the spear out through the head, and the body falls to ground. Lucifer summons soldiers to take the body away.

He walks back to Aphrodite and says, "You know Ares was about to kill my demon. You already had it dead before I could even get here."

The imp scurries in front of Aphrodite and says, "The demon was very hostile toward her. And, well, my new master did what was necessary, my king."

Lucifer looks at the imp in disgust.

29

The imp begins to back away in fear and hides behind Aphrodite.

Lucifer looks at Aphrodite and says, "In hell, we don't allow our servants to talk without being talked to first."

Aphrodite stands up straight with flames flowing through her eyes and says in a stoic tone, "Not in my realm. You may be their king, but we are on equal footing, Lucifer. If I wanted to, I could impale you too here. I am here because you said you could bring me my husband."

Lucifer gets cold shivers hearing Aphrodite talk in a serious tone. He straightens up and says in a peaceful tone, "Of course, Aphrodite. Like I said, it will take some time. I will get him here as soon as I can."

Aphrodite now has flames dancing around her finger; and she says, annoyed, "But yet you come here with just yourself and without my husband."

Lucifer quickly says, "I will arrange it. Just give me some time."

Aphrodite looks at him and says, "Very well." She sits on her throne of stone and looks at Lucifer and says, "Do not return till you have Ares with you."

Lucifer nods and then says, "He has chosen to go by his realm for a name now. He is now Violence."

Aphrodite looks at him in anguish and says, "Then I shall be known as Wrath."

Lucifer nods and walks away.

The imp comes up to Wrath and says, "I am sure he will return with your husband."

Wrath pats her lap, and the imp runs and jumps on her. She looks down at the imp and could see this imp feels safe around her. Wrath begins to pet the imp's neck and says, "If he does, I will no longer have a husband. I shall be a widow."

The imp, enjoying the massage, says in a relaxed squeak, "Why is that, my master?"

Wrath replies, "More than likely, I will kill my husband for abandoning me when I need him the most."

The imp replies, "You love him too much, my master."

Wrath smiles down at the imp and says calmly, "All is fair when it involves love and war. I now have both. Not even God knows what will happen."

The imp replies, "Yes, my master."

Wrath retorts with a sympathetic tone, "What are you called by?"

The imp looks up, confused. "I do not know what you mean, master."

Wrath looks down, confused, and states, "What is your name?"

The imp begins to look nervous.

Wrath sees the look and says, "There is no harm in the question, my little friend."

The imp begins to relax and says sheepishly, "I do not possess one. We are of no importance, master."

Wrath looks down at the imp and has a look of disgust on her face.

The imp sees the shock on her face and gets down off her lap and begins to bow.

Wrath says confusingly, "What are you doing? Come here."

The imp looks up, confused. "I thought you would not want to be in the presence of a nobody."

Wrath smiles and gets off her throne to meet the imp and says in a calm voice, "You are of importance to me." She begins scratching the imp's ear. "Let's start by me knowing, are you a boy or girl?"

The imp, enjoying the scratching, says in a sleepy voice, "We do not have genders."

Wrath looks and thinks and says, "Can I call you Cilia?"

The imp begins to shake with excitement and hops in Wrath's embrace and whispers, "Thank you, Master."

Wrath continues to hold her new friend and cradles the imp. "Call me Wrath, my new friend."

3

An infantry unit and an engineering unit are in Afghanistan. A sergeant is walking to his platoon to get them ready. He walks into six engineers mingling about. Private Wolfe sees the sergeant walk in and stands at parade rest and yells, "At ease!"

The rest of the squad gets up, and the sergeant acknowledges the gesture and says in a military tone, "At ease, soldiers." The sergeant looks around. He clears his throat and says, "We are going on patrol here soon. Keep in mind we are in season right now, so pack accordingly. Make sure we have ammo, MREs, and I don't care—bring the tent with you. I would rather have it and not need it."

Private Wolfe says, "Roger that, Sergeant. I'll bring the *Playboys*, just in case."

The sergeant looks down in disappointment and retorts with, "Private, I have seen your collection. Leave your weird shit here."

The group smiles and looks at Wolfe.

Wolfe responds, smiling, "You know you were asking me for some of that stuff not long ago."

The sergeant smiles and says, "Let's get serious here for a moment and lock it up unless it is mission related."

The tent opens, and Commander Hawke walks in.

Private Wolfe stands up and yells, "Group, attention!"

The sergeant looks at Wolfe in the position of attention and says, "Private, I don't mind it, but we do not call attention downrange. That is how we will get our officers killed." He turns to the commander, who is staring at Private Wolfe in a deadly manner. The sergeant says, "Sorry about that, ma'am. He is still learning."

She sighs and retorts, "He has been learning for three years now. Honestly, I want to start his discharge paperwork here soon if he doesn't shape up."

Wolfe says, "Permission to speak?"

She looks at him with mistrust and nods at him.

He responds, "I am in shape, 310 on my last point score."

The sergeant lowers his head in shame and moves out of her way.

She moves toward Wolfe slowly and says quietly, "You know your point scores and marksmanship of the various weapons are impressive but this"—she points at his rank—"this is pathetic."

Wolfe stays quiet.

She moves back and addresses the squad by saying, "You are going on patrol here soon, and I need to go over the ROE with this squad." She looks at Wolfe and says, "For obvious reasons." She continues, "We are in season. It's starting to warm up, and I want to remind you we are here for hearts and minds. So, soldiers, I need you to be an extension of the United States. How you react to the citizens will either make an ally or a foe, and I would rather have allies than enemies. Are we clear?"

The squad responds with a, "Hooah."

The commander signals to move out, and as Wolfe grabs his rifle and assault pack and begins to move out, she stops him and then asks the sergeant to "stick around for a moment more." They stand and wait for everyone else to leave, and she begins with stating, "Wolfe, I need you not to be trigger happy. I can see the fear in your eyes along with excitement. I just want you to know that this is real life. These people have lives and children. I want you to put yourself in their shoes and think about that."

Wolfe nods in agreement.

She looks and him with mistrust again and sighs. "What is really going on your mind?"

The sergeant tries to interject, "We know the obj—"

She cuts him off and says, "He can talk, so let him."

The sergeant looks down, almost like he is praying.

Wolfe looks her in the eye and says, "If I was in their shoes, we would not have gotten this far, and I would be waiting for the moment to rid the invaders from my land."

She looks at him with disgust and says, "Just do your job and we won't have problems, Private. I want to give you rank, but the number of counseling you have had are absurd. Help me help you."

Wolfe, still staring at her, says, "I will do my job as a soldier."

She nods and then leaves.

The sergeant looks at him and says, "You should just fuck and get it over with."

Wolfe looks at him with disgust and says, "She reminds me of a little sister, always thinking she's morally right and just. Why? Just because she went to some university and got a piece of paper that makes her benevolent."

The sergeant responds to him, "Let's just get this patrol out of the way."

Wolfe nods at the sergeant and begins to move to the Humvees.

The sergeant yells, "Mount up! Wolfe, you ride with me on the gun."

Wolfe hops in the gun and gets his stuff set up.

One of the squad members stands in front and begins to countdown. The soldier hits zero, and they all start the engines at the same time and go on their patrol.

They roll through the town and sees a bunch of people looking at them, and Wolfe sees kids looking at them with anxiety as they run inside.

Wolfe calls out, "Weapons ready. Seeing hostile behavior."

The squad turns on their alert, and Wolfe is doing his best to scan windows, looking for a surprise attack. He doesn't notice a fresh dug-up dirt pile and wheelbarrow next to the street full of rocks. The sergeant calls it out, but Wolfe is too focused on the windows to look. They get close enough, and more civilians go inside the building.

Wolfe begins to hear a stoic male tone yell, "Ambush!" He looks back and to the side, trying to find where the voice came from, but sees nothing.

The sergeant sees Wolfe looking and yells, "Do you got anything?"

Wolfe responds quickly, "Negative."

Their jammers start to pick up a signal, which is going up and down. They cross over the pile and get next to the wheelbarrow. Wolfe looks at the wheelbarrow and sees a wire running out, and before he can call it, it explodes, knocking Wolfe back inside the Humvee. Gunfire starts to unravel in a full-on firefight. Wolfe looks at the passenger side and sees another soldier is hit with shrapnel from the explosion and is dead. He can hear the bullets hitting the vehicle and see the sergeant calling for the QRF.

The sergeant looks at Wolfe and yells, "They will be here in five minutes! We need to set up a parameter!"

Wolfe nods and yells, "Son of a bitch!" He is still dazed and opens the door and points the rifle at the nearest rifle flash and starts unloading rounds. He sees the nailing to the right is not firing or even active, and Wolfe calls out, "Shift left and take the building!"

The sergeant kicks the door and starts shooting for cover fire. The squad moves in and shuts the door. Wolfe goes to the other side of the vehicle and grabs the dead soldier and drags him inside, bullets hitting around. He gets in safe. The sergeant looks around and calls for ammo check.

The squad checks and yells, "Green!" around.

Wolfe hears the faint voice again.

"Five hostiles on the third floor."

He looks at the sergeant and says, "We need to secure this building quick!"

The sergeant nods and yells, "Wolfe, take point!"

Wolfe takes position, and they stack up behind them, leaving the dead soldier. They go up one story and secure the rooms.

The sergeant says, "Let's secure the third. I got point on me."

They begin to move and make their way to the third floor and begin to hear people banging on the door, which distracts the sergeant, and an AK-47 from another door tears into the sergeant. Wolfe points his weapon at one of the sounds and unloads a mag into the door and hears a body drop.

The voice comes back. "Four more. You have thirty seconds before they breach. Move quick."

Wolfe looks and hand signals to the squad to hold and defend the stairs. They get the sergeant and start doing the best they can to stop the bleeding from multiple gunshots.

Wolfe moves to the next door and sees it start to pulse and can almost hear the heartbeats of the people inside. He kicks the door open, and gunfire starts ringing. Wolfe throws a grenade in, and he hears people start to move, and then there is an explosion. He hears the voice faintly say, "One more." He goes in weapon ready, and he hears his squad firing downstairs and the insurgents firing back. He looks more and more and sees a closet pulsing. An explosion goes off and startles Wolfe, and he fires off a couple of rounds till he hears a body drop.

The voice comes back and says, "Wrong one, but your squad needs you."

He hears a yell from one of the squad members, "Wolfe, I can't hold this much longer!"

Wolfe hustles and sees two more of his squad have been shot. The last looks at him, and a bullet tears through his neck. His body falls lifeless down the stairs. Wolfe goes to his sergeant and takes his grenade and throws it down the stairs and braces over the sergeant barely breathing. The explosion goes off, and all is silent for a second, then he hears a fifty caliber and more soldiers move. One insurgent walks behind him and sees only Wolfe alive and in shock. The insurgent pulls his knife.

Wolfe, still staring, hears the voice again, this time in an urgent manner.

"Wake the fuck up, Wolfe! You still have to protect your group. Do not drop your shield!"

He gets up and pulls his knife off his chest. He also takes his helmet off and takes a defensive stance. The insurgent charges at him, and Wolfe braces it and moves his body out of the way of the knife. Gunfire is still going on outside. The insurgent kicks Wolfe in the thigh, making him kneel. Wolfe responds by slashing his knife, making contact with the skin of the insurgent's legs, making him back up. The insurgent charges at him again, and Wolfe charges back using his legs to propel him with force. Pushing them thru the wall as they both fall two stories knocking them unconscious as the insurgents quickly see the commotion and grab the bodies away.

Wolfe is thrown in the back of an SUV supervised by and insurgent as they take him to a hideout in the mountain. He fades in and out of conscious as he is carried into a small cell. He sees a group of men approaching him talking amongst themselves. He looks up to see the man he was wrestling with as Wolfe tries to get up, now of the insurgent smacks him with the stock of his AK. Wolfe nose breaks as he is hung up on chains as the leave him there to rest. Wolfe begins to dream, as he is still in the cell but not bound. He walks around as the gate opens, Wolfe looks at the gate as he says "Hello". A cold wind comes from behind him making him shiver as it is guiding him to the outside of the gate. Wolfe walks out and sees a cold mountain bleeding crimson blood from the roof.

Wolfe is taken back on as he begins to hear "Do not fear my wolf, come." Wolfe walk thru and the blood hits him but falls on his skin but doesn't stick. Wolfe follows the cave around as he begins to see a trail of blood leading in to a circle area. Wolfe slows down and starts to slow down his breathing as he walks around it trying to figure out what is happening to him. He hears over here as he sees a shadow on the wall walking around. Wolfe stares at the shadow as he says confused "What is this." Ares responds quickly "Mesopotamia, the birth place of your blood line." Wolfe responds slowly "Is this a fever dream." Ares responds "You are in between, rest now my Wolfe."

Wolfe falls fast asleep exhausted from the day as he sleeps, he dreams of a walls bleeding. The cold but relaxing air as he looks at his body repairing quickly, he sees his wounds shut. He looks up and sees a pair of golden eyes staring at him thru the darkness. Wolfe gets a deep sleep thru the night despite his circumstances.

One of the insurgent walks to Wolfe cell and sees him sleeping deeply. The insurgent looks over Wolfe body and sees none of the gashes or wounds from yesterday. The insurgent gets opens the gate as he gets a closer look. He looks on in disbelief and slightly disturbed remembering all the myths and fables about the United States military. The insurgent quickly shuts the doors as Wolfe body animates and starts speaking

Arabic "Aaana fejeek" (you will regret this) the insurgent takes off to grab more people.

Wolfe wakes up and sees a bunch of insurgents locked on him with their weapons. He wakes up startled as he raises his hand in surrender. The insurgents start speaking to him in Arabic confusing Wolfe even more. Wolfe starts to say in a panic "I surrender". The insurgents gets more loud as they keep trying to get him to speak. They hear a door open as the insurgents begin to make way for them. One man moves past the group to Wolfe as he doesn't break eye contact with him.

The man get close enough for them to talk as the man opens up "My men say you are a demon". Wolfe looks around to them responding "I guess it depends what side of the table you are on." The man smiles at the answer and continues "The difference is my men do not heal from deep wounds in less than a day." Wolfe looks at him confused, the man recognizes his look as he helps him up letting Wolfe look down at what was his wounds. Wolfe looks and sees his body not even bruised, his cut on his abdomen is completely healed. Wolfe looks up at the man as he says "Did you heal me?" The man nods no as he walks away. Wolfe looks around and sees him leaving as he ask "please I do not know what's going on."

The man leaves the cell as he walks out with the others, leaving Wolfe alone. Ares voice comes back "We are almost there." Wolfe says out loud answering "Almost where." Ares responds "To freedom, you will not die here." Wolfe looks around "I am chained up in a cell God knows where." Wolfe looks at the corner and sees a set of eyes watching him talk to himself. Wolfe stares at the man saying "It is not what it looks like." The man continues to watch like he is enjoying the show. Wolfe nods his head as he says "Do you speak English?" The man just stares back without an idea of what he saying. This goes on for a couple of days as he slowly released of the chains allowing him to walk around the cell.

The man comes after a couple of days as he says "My men tell you speak Arabic. Is this true?" Wolfe gets up and says "I do not speak Arabic." The man smiles as he says "You said you will regret this." Wolfe looks confused as he tries to process how would he even try. The man looks at him process as he says "Either you are a good liar or you are possessed." Wolfe looks at him concerned as he says "I have no idea what you are talking about." The man responds "We shall see." He moves his hand towards Wolfe as the men string him back up. The man says "we can stop this if you remember."

Wolfe is chained up as they bring in torture tools as Wolfe sees them he starts to plead "No no no I am telling the truth." The man looks at the fear in his eyes as he smacks Wolfe making him dazed as he says "Save your strength." Wolfe focused comes back as he the man says again "how do you say you will suffer for this?" Wolfe starts to stutter as he tries to think of something "I don't know." The man. Waves his hand to another man as he punches Wolfe across the chin and the man smacks Wolfe to the other side. Wolfe vision comes back as he sees a jackal behind them standing above them the crimson eyes staring at him. The man continues to ask questions "Do you know our language?" Wolfe looks at Ares jackal form as he says "Are you ready for me to lead you." Wolfe responds to Ares "Yes." The man looks at him relieved that he is confessing to his thoughts as he says "why did you lie?" Completely unaware that Wolfe is no longer present. Ares responds "I will lend you my strength soon, do you accept my gift Wolfe?" Wolfe responds "Yes."

The man looks around as he motions to another man, the other man pulls his knife and stabs Wolfe's leg as Wolfe eyes change to a crimson red. The Wolfe looks down immediately staring at the torturer. The torture looks up and sees his gaze as he falls back fear. Wolfe pulls moving towards the torture as the chains stop him, interrogator gets out of the cell. Wolfe pulls his arm down breaking a chain as he grab the torturer by the leg and pulls him closer. The interrogator flees to alarm everyone. Wolfe pulls the other chain free as he moves the torture as he being free in fear staring at the glowing eyes. Wolfe pulls the knife out of leg and slams it in the throat of the torturer. Wolfe looks up and can see multiple heart beats moving rapidly to him. Wolfe stands up as he looks down and sees his leg wound and hands heal completely.

Wolfe moves to the door waiting for them to breach as he hears Ares say thru his own mouth "Ready?" Wolfe responds with a grunt as he feels his adrenaline hits the max. One of the insurgent quickly rushes thru the door as Wolfe grabs him throwing him the wall and ripping his AK away immediately unloading two rounds in the chest. Looking to another heart rushing towards him, he aims and quickly peaks and unloads two round striking him in the chest center mass. The insurgent drops as wolf moves over before he steps over him he puts three more rounds in him. Ares says thru Wolfe's voice "Let's have some real fun shall we?" Wolfe body involuntary moves to the ground as he a crimson enters his skin and he can feel a sudden surge of heat hit his body. He stands up as a shield appears with a chain in the other one. Ares says thru his voice "I forgot how good it feels to be in this plane." Wolfe hears sometime around the corner as the Wolfe with Ares help slings the chain striking him as it punches thru his skull. Wolfe pulls it back as he sees everyone hearts beat around the area all gathering around an exit.

Wolfe stares at the hearts beats as his starts to beat faster. Wolfe starts to look for another way as Ares says "There is only one way out, and I am running out of time here." Wolfe nods as he turns the corner holding his shield first tanking all the bullets. The shield holds strong as they start to reload, Wolfe whips the chain slicing thru flesh. Some the insurgents begin to flee as they start to believe that U.S military are demons. The last ones see the fight is lost as the drop their weapons and kneel. Ares says "Lucky timing I am out of energy, I'll be in touch." Wolfe eyes go back to being hazel as he looks at the rest of them. He thinks about it as he points outside releasing them. The insurgents grab the wounded and dead quickly as they leave.

Wolfe looks around hungry and thirsty as he looks around and sees a milky bottle as he grabs it to examine it. He uncorks it and smells the Liquorish substance and takes a swig as he feels the burn going down. He look next to it and sees a bread as he starts to eat it. Wolfe walks outside the cave and sees the last of the cars flee. He looks up and sees a small metallic object flying in a circle around his area. Wolfe walks back inside and looks around too think of what is next and process what happened. Wolfe starts to shake as the realization of his situation hits. The emotion toll starts to set in as he takes another swig of the bottle as the burn hits again. He lays down to energy that his body just exerted as he take nap to begin to rejuvenate.

He wakes up the sound of footsteps around in the cave. Wolfe stays still while he weighs his options. He begins to hear the rustling of different items as the unknown man starts to speak "You know we were watching this place for a good part of a year, and one soldier from an engineer company happens to get captured and dragged here." Wolfe begins to get up as he turns and sees a well-built older man looking over the cave. Aten turns to him holding his hand out in a hand shake "Aten, Mr. Wolfe" Wolfe takes his hand saying "Pleasure". Aten smiles continuing "So Wolfe tell me how did you do it?" Wolfe responds "If I told you, you wouldn't believe me." Aten smiles as he sees the bottle of milky liquid "what did you think of Arak?" Wolfe responds "It is no Don Julio but it's something." Aten smiles as takes a swig too "So Wolfe tell me." Wolfe Sighs as he starts to recall everything "There is a God in my head that helped in me in short he can talk to me sometimes even take control." Aten smiles "That is a bold claim but the ones you chased out of here cooperate with your story they say they captured a demon and the demon showed them what hell looks like." Wolfe looks at him even more confused as Aten continues "I had that exact look the only thing that is fascinating me is I was searching for a clue for an artifact in this area." Wolfe looks down the cave "I did not find anything then again I wasn't really looking. Whatever you want take it, it's not mine anyways."

Aten finds a seat "Do you know where you are soldier?" Wolfe responds confused "Mesopotamia?" Aten surprised responds "Did you study history or geography?" Wolfe says "the little God in my head told me earlier." Aten continues "Can you still hear him?" Wolfe shakes his head saying "no he said he needed to rest." Aten chuckles "that makes two of you." Wolfe smiles and chuckles as well "That's understatement. What about the bodies?" Aten pats Wolfe's back "They will come back as soon as we leave, they always do." He gets up and motions him to come with him. They both walk out the cave and Wolfe sees three helicopters and soldier armed and ready but not in uniform. Wolfe looks around as Aten says "I wasn't sure if you would be friendly so just in case." Wolfe follows Aten in the helicopter. Aten says to Wolfe "We just need to do a quick pit stop, don't worry your unit has already been informed." Wolfe eyes light realizing this was planned "How long have been watching" Aten responds quickly "Since they dragged you into that hole." Wolfe gets set up in the helicopter while says "What happened to my platoon anyways?" Aten looks somber as he tells the truth "They did not make it. However Hawke has been asking for you repeatedly in the name of "Accountability." Wolfe snicker "She could never just admit it that she loves me like a big brother." Aten responds "She will visit you soon but let's get you safe first… and showered." Wolfe points at him and smiles "Thank God."

They fly over cities in a black hawk and eventually land at an air base. Wolfe piles out of the helicopter and looks to the building and sees Captain Hawke standing and waiting like a statue. Wolfe can feels an uneasy knot in his stomach as he begins to walk to her. Wolfe get a couple of feet away as he drops his bag and salutes her. She shakes her head and drops the stoic stance as she hugs Wolfe glad he is alive. Captain Hawke whispers "Glad you are alive." Wolfe snickers as he says "That makes one of us." Hawke smacks his chest as she lets go and says "What happened?" Aten walks up behind them as he hears her and quickly interjects saying "Unfortunately Wolfe can not answer that just yet." Hawke looks confused as she responds "Who are you to tell me what I can and can not ask my solider." Aten looks at her with irritation "Says the Dod Captain." Hawke looks at him confused as she says "Where are your credentials sir?" Aten holds his hand out implying to look around her to the men the helicopters, he can see she is not satisfied as he pulls out a card showing he is a 2 star general. Captain Hawke looks at it and apologizes "I am sorry sir, just looking out for my soldiers." Aten face changes back to relaxed as he says "Understood. However Wolfe we need to get you back to the state side ASAP. Captain Hawke I will be sending you paperwork for the transfer of this solider to me." Captain Hawke nods "Yes sir. Will I get to see my soldier again?" Aten responds "Yes captain we are located in North Dakota is where we will be transferred to." They all says there good byes as Wolfe hugs Hawke one more time before they leave their own way.

Wolfe walks behind Aten as Aten points to a room saying "This is yours get showered and ready to move out tomorrow, chow is in two hours. Hooah?" Wolfe nods saying "Hooah" Aten walks away as Wolfe walks in to his room and immediately looks for the shower and finds it in the corner. He heads in the restroom and turns it on getting ready to shower. He gets in and closes his eyes as the water hits his face. He opens his eyes and see the shower walls are covered in blood and the shadow of Ares is on the wall. Ares speaks thru him again "Soon my wolf you will know peace." Wolfe thinks more as he gets an uneasy feeling. Ares continues "At ease solider." Wolfe blinks again and the shower goes back to normal. He looks down to see where the blood went but can only see dirty shower water taking layers of sand off of him. What was supposed to be a relaxing shower just turned into unsettling moment.

He gets out of the shower and sees a fresh set of fatigues on the bed. He begins to change into them and throwing his old clothes away in the trash. He takes a deep breath as he try to calm down. He remembers the size of what he saw, the uncanny eyes staring thru him like it was looking at his soul. He takes a deep breath and smells the food cooking.

4

Saint Michael sits on his silver throne, looking over the depths of hell and watching, making sure nothing tries to escape, when suddenly he hears a slam and an abnormal commotion in the very bottom of the pit. Saint Michael stares into the abyss till he sees an eagle head ripped off a horse's body right next to a cell. Saint Michael stands up and spreads his silver wings and drops down to the depths of hell, till he reaches another gate, and he has made it too Taurus. Saint Michael looks at the gate standing solid and glowing a silver white too. He sees a black slime appear and then take the form of a shadow.

Saint Michael sighs and says, "Go back to your hole."

The shadow becomes Lucifer, and he responds, "Come now, my dear bro."

Saint Michael draws his sword, cutting him off, and Lucifer puts his hands up and backs up and continues, "I acknowledge that we have been distant but even this is a little much."

Saint Michael stares at him, not dropping his guard.

Lucifer shrugs and says, "Very well," and returns back to slime and go away.

Saint Michael puts his hand on the door, and it opens up, and as he walks in, he sees several different abomination of earth-ending creatures. He looks ahead and sees imps and other abominations gathered around. Saint Michael pulls his sword, and it makes a ringing sound getting the attention of the group, and they back away from the scene. He walks up to body to examine it after a little view. The body twitches, and he hears a grumbling.

Saint Michael turns to the noise and sees a dark soldier's shadow. The shadows walks toward the light, and it is Atlas standing more built than ever.

Atlas looks down at the body, then back to Saint Michael and says, "This poor thing wanted to test its luck with me, and as we can see... did not go as he planned."

Saint Michael puts his sword away and says, "Atlas?"

Atlas nods and says, "I can barely recall when the last time I have heard my name said, let alone remembered."

Saint Michael responds, "When I was younger I had to learn about all the Titans."

Atlas sits down on the ground next to cell wall.

Saint Michael backs up, remembering the body right next to them.

Atlas sees his concern and says, "You have no reason to fear me. You have not transgressed me in any shape or form. I shall not hurt you. I give my word as a Titan."

Saint Michael relaxes a bit and moves a little closer and says, "The legends says you died to Hercules a long time ago."

Atlas looks at his body and says, "I wish that were true sometimes. As you can see though, I am not dead."

Saint Michael is curious, and Atlas continues to looks at him and continues, "We came to an agreement that I would come here with my brothers to spend eternity. In exchange, I would no longer have to hold the heavens."

Saint Michael looks at Atlas and sees his expression of regret, he asks Atlas, "Do you regret it?"

Atlas thinks deeply and takes a second, then finally responds, "I have had plenty of time to think on this subject, however could never really say it." He takes a deep breath. "I regret it, nor for the reason you mays think of."

Saint Michael look intrigued and takes the bait. "What do you mean?"

Atlas stands up and responds, "I see so much potential in the angel. The world with humans are doomed." Atlas takes a breath. "Angels, even though inferior to Titans, could become Titans in their own volition. However, your father is one of us, and he understood that."

Saint Michael thinks and retorts, "What do you mean angels could become Titans?"

Atlas looks Saint Michael in the eye and responds, "Your father has hindered your ability to grow, not sharing information. Like giving a plant just enough sunlight to stay alive. We, Titans, understood and shared our knowledge among us."

Saint Michael, very confused and feeling betrayed, continues to get information out of Atlas.

"Is it still possible?"

Atlas takes a seat at the bars again, and Saint Michael gets comfortable and sits next to Atlas on the other side of the bars.

Atlas lets Saint Michael get comfortable and then answers him, "It is, but you will need a Titan, and it will have to be done on earth."

Saint Michael looks down he begins to think about how to make this happen.

Atlas smiles and says, "I can feel you thinking about how to make this happen."

Saint Michael sighs and answers, "I am currently thinking what could I do with that power."

Atlas responds, "You can have true freedom until you meet someone stronger. I was made by Cronus, and I never got the chance to become what I was meant to be."

Saint Michael feels sympathy and thinks of the other angels that mock his authority.

Atlas continues, "If I may?"

Saint Michael responds, "Of course."

Atlas says, "It's nice to have someone to talk to."

Saint Michael looks at him and says, "Could you make me a Titan?"

Atlas looks at Saint Michael and states, "It is not impossible. It will be hard but not out of reach."

Saint Michael responds and says, "What would you need?"

Atlas, knowing he has Saint Michael intrigued, begins to state what he knows.

"I will need Cronus."

Saint Michael sighs and says defeated, "That is out of jurisdiction."

Atlas responds, "I figured, that is just the last piece I know where Cronus is, but I need five angel or the mask."

Saint Michael looks at him shocked, and Atlas sees the expression and states, "Calm down. The mask was not of my creation."

Saint Michael quickly asks, "How do you know of the angelic mask?"

Atlas nods his head down the hall and says, "There is a very unpleasant individual a couple of cells down. However, he know a lot of things on earth."

Saint Michael stares at Atlas, puzzled, and says, "That's not possible?"

Atlas responds, "That is a different beast entirely. However, we are running out of time."

Saint Michael looks around and can see floor starting to shake. Atlas stands up and Saint Michael stands up, Atlas towering over Saint Michael.

Atlas says quickly, "Get me out of here, and I will make you a Titan."

Saint Michael thinks and says quickly, "Me and some others, that is the only way I could make this happen."

Atlas can see the floors shaking faster, and he says, "Deal." He holds his hand out to shake on it.

Saint Michael takes his hand and shakes on it.

Then Saint Michael closes his eyes as the gate starts to spread apart. A silver light begins to break the lock as it starts to slowly open. They release their hands. Atlas steps out as Saint Michael spreads his wings and fly up to heaven.

Saint Michael lands on his throne area and paces, trying to come to terms with the deal he has just made. The anxiety and adrenaline rush are getting the better of Saint Michael. He continues to pace when he hears steps coming to him. He stops pacing and takes a seat.

Saint Peter walks into the room and stands next to Saint Michael and says, "How does it look down there?"

Saint Michael looks down, staring into the abyss.

While Saint Michael was looking, Saint Peter continues, "How is Ares?"

Saint Michael changes his view to Ares's realm and sees him ripping a spine out of an unfortunate soul and turns his head eyes fully gold, almost like he staring into Saint Michael's soul.

Saint Michael breaks the stare and says to Saint Peter, "He just ripped a spine out. I am assuming he is in his element, the dirty animal."

Saint Peter sighs and asks, "Why do you hate your brother so much, Michael?"

Saint Michael looks at him, shocked. It is the first time someone has addressed him without his title.

Saint Peter sees his face and retorts, "Relax, I have seen you since you were barely a baby."

Saint Michael takes a deep breath and finally addresses the question. "It is not that I hate him. I was made to better than him."

Saint Peter responds, "You two were meant to complement each other."

Saint Michael looks and him with confusion.

Saint Peter summons a chair out of the ground and takes a seat.

Saint Michael continues to debate the subject. "Ares is an animal who only wants war, that is not an ally nor enemy. He lives to his own will."

Saint Peter nods and asks Saint Michael, "Do you not trust his judgment."

Saint Michael, getting annoyed by the question, snaps at Saint Peter with aggression, "What is the purpose of this?"

Saint Peter calmly says, "I am just wondering why you did not believe him when he said he was innocent?"

Saint Michael looks back into the abyss and says, "His energy was all over that bloody mess."

Saint Peter sees he has overstayed his welcome and says, "That may be true. However, Ares is innocent of those crimes, and in doing poor judgment, we have lost several powerful angels."

Saint Michael, surprised, looks at Saint Peter, confused.

Saint Peter stands up and begins to walk out.

Saint Michael has been thinking of a question and finally ask Saint Peter, "Saint Peter, do you miss being a Titan?"

Saint Peter turns around and shows his ankles having wings on them. "I have never stopped being a Titan. However, they we were brutal, in constant struggle for power, even to the point where they would devour each other for the sake of power. They had no order. Your father was the one who gave me a second chance to join him on earth one last time in spirit like he did."

Saint Michael turns and thinks on the subject as Saint Peter walks out of the room.

Saint Michael sits for a minute and thinks to himself and what he about to do. He reaches into his chair and pulls out five crystal stones and looks at them. Then he stands up and stretches his wings out and dives into hell and lands in an ice-cold wasteland. He hits the ground, and ice kicks up. Saint Michael looks for Boreas and sees nothing. Eventually, he sees an ice throne with a lanky figure. Saint Michael begins to walk to him, and he takes a step, and it follows with a crack. Saint Michael looks down and see souls making up the floor frozen solid. He continues to move to Boreas.

Boreas sees Saint Michael with his icy-blue eyes. He stands up and meets Saint Michael halfway. He starts the conversation like an old friend.

"How are you, my dear friend?"

Saint Michael looks at his icy-blues eyes and smiles and responds, "My old friend indeed. I am coming to you with a proposition, my dear friend."

Boreas look intrigued by Saint Michael and says, "I cannot wait to hear it."

Saint Michael looks around and asks, "Is there a place we can sit?"

Boreas hand starts to get frosty, and an ice chair comes out of the ground, held by unfortunate souls. Saint Michael looks at it, uncomfortable, and sits down on the chair. He proceeds to get comfortable, then begins with his bargain.

"To cut things short so I can go unnoticed on my absence."

Boreas gets closer, enticed now, and asks, "What are you purposing, noble Saint Michael?"

Saint Michael leans in closer and says, "I am purposing that you follow my lead till we can freely choose where we go no farther. No rules. We can become what we were intended for."

Boreas leans back and says quietly, "There is only way to do that."

Saint Michael leans back as well. "I am well aware, but I have recently developed a new powerful friendship, and I would share my gifts with my loyal friends."

Boreas thinks for a moment and then smiles and says, "Just tell me what you need to do, my friend."

Saint Michael readjust himself and then leans in closer, then says, "We need friends, not foes, Boreas."

Boreas laughs and responds, "It will be done, my friend."

Saint Michael stands up, and Boreas follows suit. Saint Michael takes Boreas's hand and shakes it, while telling him, "I appreciate you, my friend."

Boreas responds, "Let me see what I can do first before you thank me, and off note, I am no longer Boreas."

Saint Michael looks at him, puzzled, and Boreas continues, "I am Limbo now. I am no longer an angel of God."

Saint Michael nods and reaches in his satchel, then proceeds to pull out his crystals.

Limbo looks at the crystals and asks him, confused, "What are those?"

Saint Michael looks at them and hands them to Limbo and says, "They are realm changers, undetectable by angels. I need you get me three more friends."

Limbo, staring at the crystal, nods and asks Saint Michael, "How do I use them?"

"Slam one in your hand and think of someone, and it shall to take you there for a short duration."

Limbo nods, and Saint Michael spreads his wings and flies back to heaven.

Limbo sits back on his icy throne and contemplates about how he will go about this business. He thinks on it and decides the best course of action is try to make as appealing as Saint Michael. He practices for a bit and then thinks of his old friend Demeter. He looks at one of the crystals glowing with light and slams it in his hand and is taken to a dark forest area.

Limbo looks around and see human souls gnawing on trees' blood, spewing out there mouth, but still trying to get the sweet nectar of the tree. He looks at them disgusted and moves on, looking for Demeter. He sees a woman sitting on a purple throne made of tree, and he know just who she is.

Demeter sees her old friend and stands up to greets him.

"Boreas, my old friend, how are you? Or are you like majority of us going by our realm name?"

Limbo looks at Demeter, puzzled, and asks her, "How do you know?"

Gluttony smiles ever so sassy and responds, "These humans make the best aged wine as they are trying to get even just a sip. They make me a gallon."

Limbo is still confused.

Gluttony laughs and says, "Even angels love this stuff, and in return, they give me information on what I require to know."

Limbo shrugs and says, "I require your attention. I am pressed for time."

Gluttony smiles and says, flirting, "You always have my attention, my dear friend, but what can I do for you?"

Limbo swallows and responds, "Saint Michael has requested I get a team together, and I have thought of you."

Gluttony smiles and crosses her legs and says, "I will stand by you, my dear friend."

Limbo's hand begins to glow and speeds up till it flashes, and he is put back in his realm. Limbo looks at the used crystal, and it looks like a normal rock now. He drops it and looks at a new one. He thinks of Athena and slams the crystal.

He is put high on a mountain, and he looks for her and what her gimmick is for this realm. He sees nothing, then a strong bolt of lightning hits the ground, and he sees human body parts go flying. He hears a woman grunt, and he turns and sees Athena, fair as ever, sitting on a rocky throne. He makes her way to her, and before he can get close enough, she says, "How did you get here?"

Limbo holds his hand out and shows her the crystal. He walks around to face her, and she takes a crystal of her own, then slams it with his, giving it an extended duration. She holds her hand out, pulling rocks to form a chair to face her, and she says, "Please get comfortable."

Limbo does, and he says, "Lust, I have—"

Athena cuts him off. "I am not Lust, I am still Athena now and forever. I will not take part in my brother's games. I still serve God, but apparently, I am my brother's keeper for eternity."

Limbo looks at her, and she holds a stern look. He feels so small compared to her. He responds, "Yes, Athena."

Athena retorts quickly, "Who gave you the tools of deception?"

Limbo looks at the crystal just fully glowing, and he responds, "A friend of mine and yours, I am hoping."

Athena stands up and looks over the canyon, then says, "Anyone who uses these are of evil doing."

Limbo responds, "Then why does my fair Athena have one as well?"

Athena sighs and says, "I was planning on killing my brother."

Limbo looks shocked, and she continues, "However, it would of be fruitless. Angels can harm other angels with powers down here unless Lucifer allows it, and my brother is in his favor for being the animal he is."

Limbo snaps out of it and says, "Saint Michael has plan to get us all back together."

Athena smiles and says, "He was always hungry for power, but this is new low for him."

Limbo looks scared, and Athena continues, "I shall not part take in any of this. I hope you come to your sense as well soon."

The crystal begins to glow and blink, then he is transported back to his realm. He looks at his remaining crystals and sees three left. He slams one of them and thinks of Aphrodite.

He appears in Wrath's realm. He looks around and sees a burning earth. Nothing is left. It was all charred. He sees a throne with Aphrodite petting an imp, as if is a lap pet. He takes a step, and his leg falls through. He looks to inspect the floor and sees it is being held up by unfortunate souls searing underneath the ground. One of them looks up, and the skin tears as if is melted together. The soul reaches for

Limbo's leg. Limbo reacts and freezes the hole, then makes an icy path toward Aphrodite. He continues to walk. He forgot how beautiful she is, a perfect balance of good attributes. He starts to slow down his pace as he gets closer, unsure of himself, as he begins to feel intimidated.

He finally steps up to her and tries to say a word, and he gets tongue-tied.

"Aphrodite, Wrath…deal?"

She looks at him very confused and begins to laugh. He looks ashamed, and she gets up and says, "Let's try this again."

Limbo recoups his thoughts and says, "Do you prefer Aphrodite or Wrath?"

Aphrodite looks at the imp and says in a calm voice, "Well, what do you think?"

The imp immediately says, "Wrath."

Limbo looks at the imp and says, "What is that?"

The imp looks at her master, ashamed, and Wrath looks at limbo with rage.

Limbo begins to start and apologize, but it is too late. She has burnt his ice, and he struggled with souls beneath his feet. He begins to plead.

"I apologize. This has been devastating from the beginning. I bring word from Saint Michael."

Wrath rolls her eyes and lift him up and throws him on the ground. Wrath walks over and says in aggressive tone, "I want nothing to do with the brothers again."

Limbo looks at his crystal, and it begins to flash. He shakes his head, and the crystal finishes putting him back in his realm. He looks at the last two and says out loud but begrudgingly, "Let's try Ares."

He slams the crystal and thinks of Ares, and he is in a plain wasteland. He looks around and sees body parts scattered everywhere. He looks at a severed head. The eyes are staring at Limbo, and Limbo looks back into the bloodshot brown eyes.

Limbo, grossed out, says, "Why is he such an animal?"

The eyes blink, and Limbo is startled and takes a step back, realizing that the body is still alive. A severed hand grabs Limbo's leg. Grasping for mercy, he freaks out and freezes it. He hears a yell like ten thousand soldiers yelling. He looks up and sees a spear-like object coming his way. He quickly tries to find his other crystal, jumbling through his satchel. He hears a skull crack and feels parts of the skull hit his chest. Limbo looks where the head was and sees that it is gone and the hand has stopped grabbing and lies lifeless.

Ares comes up behind him as silent as death and startles Limbo.

"What are you doing here?"

Limbo is nervous and unsure about what to say after feeling like he is under attack.

Ares grows impatient and pulls a sword and says, "I suggest you leave." Ares walks away back to a shack.

Limbo says, "Ares, I have a proposition for you."

Ares aggressively turns around and throws his sword next to Limbo's feet and says, "There are no deals between wolfs and lambs."

Limbo takes the crystal and slams it back to his realm.

Ares turns around and heads back to his shack and sees his imp coming out to see what the commotion was about.

The imp says, "What has happened, my master?"

Ares looks at the imp and waves to walk with him. Ares walks to his throne, which is made of blood and bones, and says, "Someone wanting to make a deal."

The imp looks confused, and Ares follows up, "We are working on our deal, my servant."

The imp nods and waits for Ares to say something. Ares looks a glass orb and sees Wolfe has been transported to his cell and has been questioned.

Ares says stoically to the servant, "Roll out my gear. It is almost time to make my own deal with someone more suitable."

The imp hurries to a table and rolls it out, showing him everything from swords, spears, shields, and his armor.

Ares addresses it with great care and inspects the swords first. Ares runs his finger over the blade, and it cuts him. He looks at the servant, and the imp bows, then states, "Apologies, my master."

Ares smiles and says, "None needed. I am proud of you, my servant."

The imp looks up, shocked to hear Ares being positive for once to him.

Ares continues, "You have heeded my training well, and that's all I can ask for."

The imp tail starts to move, and Ares looks at it. Ares smiles, moves his throne closer, and says, "Proceed on the rest of my items."

The imp goes over the swords and says, "I have imprinted your touch. Any other life-form that touches this, except for me and you, will trigger spikes that come out of the hand."

Ares smiles, and the imp continues, "I tried to do everything, but the metal cannot be trained to be the metal you used when you were Thor."

Ares says sternly, "That's unfortunate. However, I did enjoy those humans."

The imp says, "However you can send the weapons back here for maintenance when needed."

Ares waves it, and the imp continues, "The armor scales with your power as well."

Ares looks confused and says, "How did you manage to do that?"

The imp replies, "Hell's metal. I tried to replicate holy metal. It is not a one-to-one comparison. However, I don't think you will be taking on angelic forces while you are where you need to be."

Ares says sternly, "Be prepared for everything."

The imp nods and says, "Forgive me, my master. This was the best I could do, with the material I have."

Ares looks annoyed and says, angered, "It is too late to rectify mistakes. I will make do."

The imp bows, and Ares gets up and look over the breastplate and see two wolves pulling on Ankh. He goes over the pattern and says quietly, "This is a nice touch."

The imp retorts, "A true warlord armor, my master."

Ares looks at the armor and says, "Have it two knife sitting on the chest."

The imp nods, and Ares walks to his throne and says, "I have something for in my absence."

The imp looks confused. In all his time here, he has never given any gifts to the imp. The imp looks nervously toward Ares pulling something out, and he sees that Ares has made a little version of his throne for the imp. Ares puts down and awaits to see the imp take his seat.

Ares says, "This seat you shall rule till I am back."

The imp takes a seat and hears a squish, and Ares says, "I would wait for it to dry, I just pulled a soul apart to make this moments ago."

The imp gets up and says, "Thank you, Master."

Ares nods to him off and sits on his throne and contemplates how he will do in the world and what could possibly come. He feels his chest where he keeps his wedding ring and can feel her heat coming from it as he thinks of her.

In Wrath's realm, she sits in her stone throne and thinks on Limbo coming back to offer such a proposition that she ponders. Who else has he offered? How many other angels are in hell? Does he think of me? She feels her ring on her chest as it starts to vibrate with crimson energy. She closes her eyes and can still see him as clear as day the way he smells and talks. She continues and eventually begins to smile at the thought of him but is interrupted by Cilia as she scurries through the door and climbs on Wrath's lap. Wraths focus is broken as she looks down, irritated. Cilia looks sheepishly and ashamed.

Wrath recaptures her mind and says, "I apologize for the look. I was just—"

Cilia responds, "It's okay. I am sure he misses you too, Wrath."

Wrath looks at Cilia in anger but can't help but to blush as the imp giggles.

5

Wolfe, lying on a couch in his PT uniform, is being asked a question by a stuck-up studious therapist.

"How have you been, Wolfe?"

Wolfe rolls his eyes and sits up, and therapist looks at him with sympathy.

Wolfe responds while looking him in the eye, "Why must we do this? At this point, I wanna ask for my execution order."

The therapist sighs and responds, "It is part of the court agreement. We are just checking your mental stability."

Wolfe looks at him with disgust and says, "What do you mean my mental stability? I was sentenced to death, and I want my part of the deal."

The therapist responds, "Ever since you got here, you have been…" He takes a pause and continues uncooperative, hostile, belittling the staff. "For the love of God, Wolfe, I am your fourth therapist."

Wolfe looks around and sees a dictionary and gets up.

The therapist asks, "Where are you going, Wolfe?"

Wolfe grabs the dictionary, and the therapist says shamefully, "What word do you need help with?"

Wolfe responds arrogantly, "None of them. However, back to your point though." Wolfe continues to search for a word while talking still. "The last two therapist were very much like you, never knew what it was like outside of Daddy's and Mom's money."

The therapist looks at him with a sour look.

Wolfe continues, "Don't worry, I am not judging you that. However, what I will say is, you are like this word." He lays the dictionary down and points to a word.

The therapist looks at the word "parasite." The therapist doesn't rise to the bait that Wolfe is setting for him, and the therapist continues, "It does not matter what you think of me or what I think of you."

Wolfe realizes he isn't getting rid of him with insults and might have to switch to more drastic measures of avoidance.

Wolfe switches up his tone and says calmly, "I am growing weary of this, Harvard. Tell me what you want to know so I may leave to await for my day of execution."

The therapist looks through his notes and finds something interesting from the last therapist's report about Wolf's night terrors.

The therapist ask him, "How are the night terrors, and what are they about?"

Wolfe looks at him confused and says, "You want to know about my dreams?"

The therapist nods and says calmly, "Very much so."

Wolfe begins to hear the voice again.

"It is time. I do not care how you do, but I need you to get to write down 'crimson' and 'mask.'"

Wolfe looks at him, then begins to taste blood in his mouth.

The voice come back in and says, "I like where this is going."

Wolfe bites his tongue, letting the blood flow, and smiles with blood on his teeth.

The therapist sees this happening and calls for the guards.

Wolfe holds up a finger, as in, "Just a minute."

The therapist stops the guards for a moment.

Wolfe lets the blood flow in his mouth and says while spewing blood from his mouth, "I taste blood in my dreams. Many have tried to live my life, and all have failed. I have a birthright that is calling to me. What I need you to write down, and I apologize in advance."

The therapist looks confused.

Then Wolfe throws the dictionary at him, and the guards grabs Wolfe. Wolfe struggles and yells, "I see mask made of crimson blood!

You hear me, Harvard. A mask made out of crimson blood, you fucking parasite!"

They escort Wolfe out, and the therapist writes down everything on his laptop and files his report. He sends it to his library of his other clients.

The guards throw Wolfe in the cell. He hits his head on the bunk and falls down, passed out.

—⁓—

Director Aten is standing behind bullet-proof glass watching Dr. Smith give another top-tier soldier his next objective. Director looks at the candidate folder's profile and rereads all of his triumphs and history. The doctor finishes up and gets the soldier fired up. The soldier takes a seat, and the doctor puts restraints on and straps him the chair, then proceeds to join Aten in the observation chamber.

Aten looks at the doctor and asks, "How did you get him fired up like that?"

The doctor smugly says, "It was not an easy sell. I tried telling him the science, and it was going over his head."

Aten looks at him confused.

The doctor sees his face and says, "That exact look."

Aten replies, "So why is so hooah about this."

The doctor replies, "I told him I am going to try to make him into Captain America."

Aten looks disgusted.

The doctor says, "It works on all the other candidates too. I do not understand."

Aten just shakes his head and hops on the intercom and tells the soldier, "Secure the mask on your face."

The soldier looks like he has just seen a ghost and hesitates in doing the action.

Aten repeats himself, "Secure the mask, Lieutenant."

The soldier does as commanded, and he shot back in his chair as the doctor looks at his vitals.

The doctor gives his reading to Aten. "Internal temp is rising but still survivable."

Aten watches like a hawk as his veins begins to glow a crimson red and the soldier screams in pain.

"Crimson!"

Aten grabs the intercom and says, "What?"

The soldier yells, "Wolfe," as he struggles to survive.

The doctor calls, "His heart rate is 180 and climbing."

Aten looks at the soldier, and to his surprise, the soldier start screaming, "I'm sorry! Please...please!" The soldier looks like someone has stolen his soul, and he stands up, eyes glowing crimson, and he says with a different voice pattern, staring at the window like it he sees their souls and says, "Lupum me adducere." Then the body explodes, and chunks fly everywhere. The aftermath looks like a version of Ares's realm.

The doctor looks at Aten, and Aten slams his hands on the desk. He states, "We worked on this subject alone for almost a year. Put him through everything—pain, torture, and harsh conditions, just to send him to die."

The doctor stares at the chair, amazed.

Aten yells at him, "Wake up."

The doctor looks at him and says, "What was that?"

Aten calms down and says, "What do you mean?"

The doctor pulls the audio from Ares and plays it back.

Aten watches and says, "It gibberish."

The doctor looks at Aten and says, "I do not believe it to be so."

The doctor pulls up the audio from the soldier and compares them.

Aten looks amazed, then asks, "What is it?"

The doctor pulls up a search engine, and Aten looks at the doctor like he is pulling a prank on him. The doctor throws in translate, and it translate to "Bring me my wolf." The doctor reads out loud, "Bring me my wolf."

Aten looks confused, and the doctor thinks for a minute and says, "You remember that trial we went to on our way to DC?"

Aten thinks and replies, "Yes, we were not even supposed to be there, but our flight got canceled."

The doctor thinks more on it and says, "What is that is the person we need. His name was Wolfe."

The director looks at him in bewilderment and says, "Its best shot we got."

The doctor replies, "Call the senator that funded this. I will bet my life we got something to show them."

Aten looks at the doctor in a serious manner and then sighs. "Either way, if you are right, this cursed death trap comes to end, or it comes to an end because we did it."

The doctor looks at him, seeing the director burdened with guilt, and the doctor says, "I'll make the calls."

Aten says, "I should do it. I will get them here. Just make sure we get Wolfe. Let's pray and hope he is not dead."

The doctor pulls up his profile and sees the word "insane" and reads the last word of "crimson" and "mask." The doctor smiles and says, "Hang in there, Wolfe. We are coming for you."

— ∞ —

Wolfe, sitting on his bunk in his cell, sees the therapist and several guards coming his way. They stop at his cell, and the guards open it up. The therapist walks in and looks at Wolfe.

Wolfe starts, "What do you want, Harvard?"

The therapist stares at him, unamused by his comment, and answers him, "We are left with a choice, Wolfe."

Wolfe looks at him disgusted and growls, "What choice is that?"

The therapist continues, "We can either stay here where we can work on your delusions…" The therapist sees Wolfe's notebook. It is covered in spartan helmets and crosses.

Wolfe brings the therapist back to conversation, "Or we could?"

The therapist snaps out of it and continues, "Some higher-ups have asked for you personally to be retrieved and brought to their location."

Wolfe looks at the therapist and responds, "Where would be this new location?"

The therapist sees a pile of unopened mail from his commander. The therapist walks over and grabs the mail and starts sorting it, then says, "Why haven't you opened them yet, Wolfe?"

Wolfe looks at him, untrusting, and says with a smile, "It is best if people think I am gone."

The therapist shifts his view back to Wolfe and says, "What will it be, Wolfe?"

Wolfe smiles and says, "As fun as I think it would be here talking about flash card, dreams, and my feelings, I suppose it would be rude for me not accept an invitation. See, my good friend, I am with honor and respect…you know, something you could only hope to dream about."

The therapist keeps a straight face and says, "Very well. You ship out tomorrow."

The therapist begins to walk away, and Wolfe says, "Hey, Harvard."

The therapist stops and looks at Wolfe.

Wolfe says, "Out of all my therapists, you were my favorite by far."

The therapist smiles a bit and signals to the guards to take him.

They go in and strap him down, and Wolfe yells, "What the fuck are you doing, faggot?"

They inject him with a sedation to put him in a coma-like state and begin to move him away.

The therapist comes back and takes one of the letters and walks back to his office.

—✺—

The next day arrives, and Wolfe wakes up earlier than normal and gets dressed. He hears the voice again.

"They are trying to find my chosen."

Wolfe stands, then sits and looks in the mirror. He sees a big dark figure behind, moving around. He stands still and watches as the voice continues to speak.

"Why do human always manage to find a way to get in their own way? My father gave humans paradise, and they still managed to make a mockery of it."

Wolfe turns around slowly and sees nothing. He looks around, confused and scared as the voice continues.

"Fret not, you cannot see me yet. At least, in this plane of existence. However, we shall meet soon, my wolf."

The voice goes away as several guards come to the door and toss in clothes and command him, "Get dressed, Wolfe."

Wolfe does as commanded.

As soon as he finishes dressing, the guard enters the cell and puts him in a straightjacket and blindfold.

Wolfe sarcastically says, "Usually, I have to pay extra for this."

The guards looks at each other and nods as one of them punches Wolfe in the jaw, knocking him out.

The guard that is watching says to the other one, "Fucking, finally, we shut him up."

The other guards laughs as they load Wolfe in the transport to take him.

—⚏—

Aten and the doctor greet their guest just arriving to watch the fruits of their labor finally come to fruition. The honored guests arrive, and they are escorted to a briefing room.

Aten and the doctor shake their hands till an old warmonger arrives and goes to shake Aten's hand.

Then senator takes his hand and says passively to Aten, "We were thinking about pulling funds from this project, but if this works out"—the senator leans in closer—"we got a lot countries and money to make money off."

Aten looks at him disgusted in the inside but nods his head, and the senator continues trying to get reaction from Aten.

"War is good for the pockets."

Aten gives him the emotion he wants to see and says, "Yes, it is, Senator. And I can't wait to benefit off the animals."

The senator looks happy and replies, "They are animal, aren't they? If only if they had a mind like ours, Aten, maybe they would understand where they stand on the food chain."

Aten nods and is done with the conversation as he take a seat to listen to the brief.

The senator takes a seat and listens to the presentation.

Aten looks to the doctor to begin, and the doctor grabs a remote and begins with, "Hello, esteemed guest and investors, we are here to show the fruits of our research." He turns on the projector and play the last subject. "We had an issue of finding a proper host to take the energy of the mask."

The video show the soldier trying to harness the crimson in his veins and begins to struggle. The doctor pauses it and says, "We can see right here is, the soldier cannot hold the energy as it surges through him."

One of the guests asks, "What is the energy type?"

The doctor responds, "We believe it to radioactive."

The guest asks, "Believe?"

The doctor responds cautiously, "We haven't had enough information to extract from the subject."

The guest asks again, "So you don't have a finished product?"

Aten takes the question and says sternly, "Not yet, but we will, and we are so confident that we wanted you people that believe in our work to see it firsthand."

The senator retorts, "What makes you so sure?"

Aten looks to the doctor, then nods to continue the video. He does so, and the guests' eyes are glued to the presentation as the soldier on the video stands up and says, "Lupum me adducere."

The senator looks intrigued, and then the body explodes, and the doctor ends the presentation.

One of the guests asks, concerned, "Where did he go?"

Aten says, knowing the senator is watching, "He is no longer with us."

The senator replies to the investor, "These trials are just how things need to be done to protect the land of the free. He died with honor. It shall not be in vain."

The investor looks disgusted in his answer.

Aten continues, "We have the proper subject." He pulls up Wolfe's picture.

The guests gaze at Wolfe's mug shot, and one of them asks, "Is he a criminal?"

Aten sighs and says, "Yes, he is a war criminal."

The senator snickers, and the guests looks at him, and one of them looks back at Aten.

"What if the same thing happens to this soldier as the last?"

The senator replies, "He is a war criminal probably waiting on death row. At least, if he dies here, he died doing some good."

The doctor says, "We are just letting you know what is going on, and we do have rooms and food for you. Wolfe shall be here by the end of tonight and prepped for tomorrow."

The guys get up, and soldiers walk in with envelops with names on them and find the perspective person.

One of the guest gets up and makes his way to Aten and says, "How do you sleep at night?"

Aten looks at him and responds, "Not very well. I'm hoping that this is the end."

The guest can see the torture in his eyes and nods, then walks to his room.

One of the soldier walks and whispers to the doctor.

The doctor holds his watch up and checks the time, then makes his way to Aten, then whispers, "He is here."

Aten and the doctor walk away.

—ᜃ—

Aten and the doctor see a security van arrive, and two guards come out of the van and open the door. Wolfe begins to step out, shackled completely, wearing a face mask to prevent biting. The guards take the blindfold. Wolfe looks around and sees a camera and stares at it, almost piercing all their souls.

The guards bring Wolfe to the briefing room as Aten walks over to Wolfe and examines Wolfe's state. Aten looks Wolfe in his eyes as Wolfe stares back, untrusting.

Aten looks at the guards and asks, "Why is he shackled in this condition?"

One of the muscular guards responds, "He is a loose cannon. He spits blood in the face of the therapist that work at our facility."

Aten looks at the doctor, disapproving, and the doctor states, "It is what we need, a fighter not a soldier."

Wolfe gives the doctor a death stare, making him uncomfortable.

Aten looks at the guards and commands, "Release him. He will be stupid to do anything here. Especially since something here is waiting for him."

The guards ask in unison, "Release him?"

Aten looks at them menacingly, then says, "Did I not say correctly? Or you two just hard of hearing?"

The guards look at Aten, and one of them removes Wolfe's shackles.

Aten watches, socially reading Wolfe's movements.

Wolfe becomes full unshackled and takes a deep breath, then says, "I have missed the fresh air."

Aten moves closer and responds, "I just want you to know, by technicality, you are dead." Aten looks at the doctor, then signals to him to give him a package.

The doctor slowly moves and hands Wolfe a package.

Wolfe opens it and sees a death certificate. He looks confused and asks, "Are you private sector or government?"

Aten replies, "We are off the grid. We do not exist, and now neither do you."

Wolfe responds, "So what would you have me do?"

The doctor chimes in, "We would have you put on a mask."

Wolfe looks at him confused and dumbfounded, then asks, "A mask?"

Aten and the doctor realize how idiotic that sounded. Aten sighs then says, "Yes, a mask."

Wolfe, still confused, states, "What kind of mask?"

The doctor says, "If I am correct, it's your mask, another being has called for specifically."

Wolfe looks around.

Aten asks, "What are you looking for?"

Wolfe smiles and says, "To see what drugs you guys got here."

Aten smirks and says, "You will see," then nods to Wolfe to follow.

They walk in to the chamber where the soldier died.

Wolfe looks around and begins to feel a cold. "What happened here?"

Aten looks at him confused and looks around for traces of blood. He doesn't see any. He asks Wolfe, "What do you mean?"

Wolfe responds, "It feels like death in here."

The doctor looks at Wolfe amazed and pulls out a notebook and starts writing down notes.

Wolfe sees the doctor writing, and he asks, "What are you doing?"

The doctor smiles and says, "We are making history." The doctor walks away to grab something.

Wolfe becomes on guard, then says, "I don't know what this is, but I am not interested in your sex dungeon with whatever you Hollywood freaks are into."

Aten looks at Wolfe in disgust and responds aggressively, "We are not making you do anything of that nature. Just wait for Smith to get back, then you can make your choice."

The doctor comes back in with a briefcase and places it on the desk, then opens it up, revealing a mask.

The lights flicker, and the room becomes cold. They look around to see what has happened. The doctor begins writing down notes as Wolfe walks over to the mask and sees the mask in his dreams. He examines the cold crimson polished mask with cross on the top and a sword, a spartan helmet on the cheeks.

Wolfe gets pale and asks, "Where did you find this?"

Aten responds, "We acquired it from the Vatican."

Wolfe goes to reach for it, and he hears the voice yell at him in his head, "Do not touch it yet. Wait for tomorrow. There is someone here that need a lesson."

Wolfe pulls his hand back and says, "I will participate in this."

Aten nods, and the doctor smiles, then hands Wolfe a packet, saying, "Your room number is in there and a map layout of the facility. Feel free to get a hot meal and a shower. We also have a change of clothes for you in the room, so choose what you will."

Wolfe nods and walks away, leaving the doctor and Aten.

The doctor smiles at Aten. Aten can't help but to smile back, knowing they have what they are looking for.

Wolfe makes his way to his room and turns on the shower and lets it warm up as it has been awhile since he has showered that wasn't supervised. He begins to hear the voice again.

"We are close, Wolfe. You have nothing to fear but fear herself."

Wolfe looks around to see if anyone else is in the room, and the voice comes back.

"They are watching. I want a little more lay of the land. Take your shower and let's get a hot meal. You have earned it."

Wolfe stands up and goes into the bathroom. As he opens the door, he sees a towering figure with the head of jackal. He stumbles and falls back, startled. He blinks, and it is gone. He regains himself and takes a shower cautiously. He gets out of the shower paranoid and begins to inspect the set of clothes and comes across a plain black T-shirt and black cargo pants. He looks for some shoes and finds a pair of black military boots and black long socks. He gets dressed, and he looks in the mirror and see himself looking almost human again.

Then the voice come back, demanding, "Rip the right sleeve off."

Wolfe looks confused and asks, "Why?"

The voice continues to protest, "Because we do not bear the mark of Lucifer."

Wolfe's eyes widen, and he rips the right sleeve. He takes look and realizes this will look weird, but he thinks about the tall figure in the door and continues.

He walks into the cafeteria and sees the other guests and guards there. He works his way to the line and sees the buffet of all-American food. His mouth begins to salivate at the thought of a burger. He quickly rushes to the burger spot.

The cook asks, "How would you like you burger, sir?"

Wolfe is confused as it been awhile since he has been treated as human, let alone called sir.

The cook repeats as he in a hurry, "Sir?"

Wolfe quickly responds, "Rare, please."

The cooks nods and makes his burger.

Wolfe is too focused on the food that he does not noticed people staring including one individual in particular. He looks back and sees the senator eyeing him up. Wolfe turns back around and waits for his food, then finds an empty table. He takes a seat, and he feels the senator get up and walk toward him. Wolfe does not break contact with the burger as the senator takes a seat with him.

The senator smiles and asks, "How is it?"

Wolfe grunts in approval.

The senator continues, "Are you going to be the one they are experimenting on?"

Wolfe, annoyed, looks up and says, "Yes, I am."

The senator smiles and says, "Good. I hope we can do some business when you are done here. I can make you a very rich man."

Wolfe looks up and says, "I am sure we will talk later."

The senator says, "Good. I shall wait for the time." Then he leaves.

Wolfe hears the voice again.

"What a scum of this earth. Politicians in Latin means multiple blood-sucking parasites."

Wolfe smiles in delight, and he hears the voice again.

"Enjoy your day. We got a big one tomorrow, my wolf."

6

The next day comes around, and Aten and the doctor go to cafeteria to get ready for the day. As they turn the corner, they see Wolfe already grabbing his coffee and getting his breakfast. Aten looks at his watch, and it reads 5:55.

He looks back at Wolfe and says, "Your assignment is not till 0900."

Wolfe takes a sip and replies, "Indeed, however PT is 0630."

The doctor looks confused and responds, "That life is behind you, Wolfe."

Wolfe looks at the doctor and states, "Maybe for you. This is how I go out though." Wolfe begins to walk away, eating, and takes a seat at an empty table.

Aten looks at the doctor, and the doctor shrugs and goes to grabs his food as Aten follows. Aten grabs his food and heads back into the doctor's labs as the doctor follows.

The doctor shuts the door and immediately says, "I don't believe working out beforehand is the correct action."

Aten chomps is food and swallows, then retorts, "I believe what you said, Doctor."

The doctor turns confused and ask quietly, "What do you mean?"

Aten takes a sip and says, "We have been going at this as a soldier would. However, all of them relied on us to push them. I think I am starting to get that Wolfe is anything but a soldier. He is a warrior."

The doctor takes a seat and replies, "What is the difference? I have never been in the field nor even held a gun."

Aten continues, "A soldier is taught how to fight, and he does so like a machine. A warrior is someone who lives for the blood and sweat. That is his whole purpose, not money nor fame, just blood."

The doctor tries to understand, and Aten continues, "He does it because he yearns for the war. Most soldiers just want to do their time and get there benefits, then leave. Wolfe is one of those rare occasions that he does not care for the money benefits or anything monetary. His whole goal is to be where the suffering is."

The doctor looks even more confused; and Aten, trying to make sense of it, says, "He is programmed that way."

The doctor's eyes light up, and Aten shakes his head. They continue to watch the cameras as Wolfe is bench pressing in the weight room.

Aten says, "I need to go brief the guest. Please keep a watch on him and let me know if he tries to escape."

The doctor nods as Aten walks away. He stares at Wolfe and starts writing down notes, when he feels a cold breeze hits his back, giving him the cold shivers.

Wolfe, pushing the weights, hears the voice.

"The doctor is weird. He is watching you."

Wolfe continues and ends his set and flips off the camera.

The doctor does not find this amusing in the slightest and continues to watch.

—◊◊◊—

The time comes for the trial, and Aten goes to the two-way mirror and sets them behind the bullet-proof glass, and he says, "Welcome to history. Ever since we knew about these items, we have never had the privilege of seeing one in action. Well, today, folks, we shall see it and hope we have answer for all warfare, helping us push justice and peace in the world."

Aten walks away to join the doctor and Wolfe as the doctor is briefing Wolfe about what is about to happen.

Aten comes in and hears, "This energy is possibly radioactive, so try to be still and let your natural emotion come out. I found that it is the best way to avoid struggling."

Wolfe stares at him with astonishment. Wolfe replies to the verbal garbage, "Can you repeat that last part?"

The doctor says in the same way. "Let your natural emotions come out. I found that it is the best way to avoid struggling."

Wolfe giggles a little bit and says, "Its sounds stupid."

Aten steps in and starts to state, "We got a lot brass and higher-ups watching you right now, Wolfe."

Wolfe responds, "Well, let's give them a show to remember."

Aten smiles and nods, then looks at the doctor.

The doctor nods and says, "We are green light. I'll shall bring it you, Wolfe."

Wolfe sits back in the chair and takes a deep breath and prepares for what will come.

Aten walks back to the guest and says, "We are about to begin, gentlemen."

The guests watch Wolfe with great anticipation. Some lean forward. The senator watches with great hope. The doctor brings in the mask and sets it in front of Wolfe, and Wolfe looks at it then asks, "Will this hurt?"

The doctor says, "More than likely, Wolfe."

Wolfe smiles and touches the mask and says, "Good."

The doctor gives a thumbs-up, signaling he is ready to go, and the doctor walks back to the other guests.

Aten takes the intercom and says, "In case of this fails, any last word, Wolfe?"

Wolfe thinks and says, "May God have mercy on us."

Aten replies, "Amen." Then he proceeds to says, "You got the green light, Wolfe."

Wolfe grabs the mask and begins to put it on. It feels natural putting it on, like he has done this a thousand time. He hears the voice again.

"Let us begin on our terms, my wolf."

The mask grabs on to Wolfe's face and gets sucked on. Wolfe relaxes and sits back. The crimson begins to set in to his view. It flows from the head and works its way to rest of the body.

Aten looks at the doctor, shouting, "What is the vitals?"

The doctor looks confused and says, "They are normal, like he is resting."

Aten gets on the intercom and says, "Wolfe!"

The doctor says, "He is in a coma-like state. Leave him."

Aten backs up and begins to fear the worst.

Wolfe enters his dream state and looks around at the low-hanging sun in a field of reeds.

Ares pops out of the fields in his jackal angelic state as his jewels on his head shine like stars. Wolfe looks and is immediately started by the giant bejeweled jackal with gold and crimson eyes glaring at him as if he was prey. Ares walks closer so Wolfe can hear him without him yelling.

"Finally, my lupus. Come, we have a lot to do and not a lot of time to do it." Ares turns and starts walking and says, "If you have any question, now is an adequate time to ask."

Wolfe looks around, not sure where to begin, so he asks, "Where are we?"

Ares responds, "The afterlife. I am taking you to what we yearn for, my dear warrior."

Wolfe responds, "What is I yearn for?"

Ares turns his head, eyes glowing, then says, "For battle with competition." Ares walks over a hill and looks down to a huge tavern. Ares says happily, "You will be in Valhalla if you can past my test, my lupus."

Wolfe looks down at warriors drinking and feasting. For the first time, he sees a place he wants to be and call it home.

Ares smiles at it too, missing his old life. He feels his chest and caress a ring in a chain, thinking of Aphrodite. Ares comes back to and taps Wolfe to follow. He leads Wolfe to a graveyard and stops by the first stone. It reads, "David." Ares puts his hand on the grave, and the dirt begins to fall down to it.

Wolfe watches with amazement as he looks at it.

Ares pushes him in.

Wolfe falls and lands in a different area. He looks around and sees a massive army. He feels something in his hand. He looks and sees it is a string.

He thinks, *What is this?*

He hears Ares's voice.

"It is the first time my work is recorded by humanity. Focus now."

Wolfe looks at the army and sees a behemoth of a man walking past soldiers as they cheer him, chanting "Goliath!"

Wolfe looks at him. Goliath is wielding a sword and shield. Wolfe gulps as he looks down to see he only has a string.

Ares's voice becomes clear again.

"Can you think on your feet to obtain blood and glory?"

Wolfe begins to look around and finds a stone. He picks it up and throws it as hard as he can at the beast. It hits his chest plate.

Everything goes silent, and the crowd starts laughing, including Goliath.

The voice comes back, commanding, "What was that?"

Wolfe looks around for a sword, shield, rifle, anything to help him. He only has a leather string.

Goliath starts to taunt Wolfe.

Ares's voice comes in. "May I offer you some guidance?"

Wolfe pleads, "Please."

Ares's voice come back. "Grab the stone and put it in the sling and then throw it, you imbecile."

Wolfe finds another stone.

Goliath sees Wolfe going for another stone and begins to laugh again.

Wolfe finds a notch, then places the stone and starts to wind up. He hurtles the stone at Goliath's head, crushing the front lobe of his brain. Goliath slowly falls dead as the soldiers watch.

Ares's voice comes back. "See how I see the world."

One of Wolfe's eyes begin to burn and turn gold mixed with crimson. Wolfe looks at the army and can see heartbeats and nervous systems flaring.

Ares's voice come back. "Do you see their heart right now? How it is slow?"

Wolfe nods.

Ares replies, "That is what grief looks like. Beautiful, isn't it?"

Ares pulls Wolfe out of the grave.

Wolfe comes back to the graveyard in shock. He says, "What was that? Who are you?" Wolfe falls over, panicking, as Ares walks over, towering over him.

He says, "That was a memory nothing, more nothing less, and I am Ares, the angel of war. Condemned angel but nevertheless still an angel."

Aten and the guest are watching the crimson flow through Wolfe's veins.

One of the guests speaks up and says, "What is going on right now, Doctor?"

The doctor looks back for a brief second and says, "Patience, it has only been…" The doctor looks at his watch and sees only thirty seconds have gone by and continues, "Thirty seconds, sir."

The guest protests, "I asked what is going on. What are we watching?"

Aten turns around and calmly says, "The mask is a doorway, and it is challenging Wolfe to whatever its will is. Usually by now, the subject would have exploded into chunks, but as you can see, he is in a calm state. We can almost declare that this is going very well."

Wolfe's hand begin to twitch, and his heart rate spikes. The doctor sees it and calls for Aten's attention.

"Aten, we have something."

Aten rushes to his screen and see Wolfe's heart rate jumped to 130 for a second. Aten looks at the jump, then back at Wolfe and mutters, "Come on, Wolfe."

Wolfe gets excited to see the famous gravestone that reads, "Achilles"

Ares stops his hand and says, "Yes, I embodied him for his last war for my love."

Wolfe looks confused, and Ares realizes he had said too much and puts his hand on the grave. The dirt begins to fall in, and Ares's hand goes to Wolfe's shoulder, then he tosses him in the grave again.

Wolfe gathers his thoughts as he is lying down in the ground. He hears someone next to him scream, "My lord, what shall we do?" as blood seeps in a field of swords and shields clashing. Wolfe looks down and sees an all-black helmet, and he examines his armor and see it is all black.

He thinks, *What is this?*

Ares voice come back and says, "This is my story of love and war. You are among one of the greatest unit of human history, true Wolfe."

The warrior screams again, "My lord, what shall we do?"

Wolfe stands up and look the bloodied soldier up and down and asks, "What do you believe me to do?"

The warrior quickly says, "We get our vengeance, Lord. They took Patriculus from you, my lord."

Wolfe thinks, *Why does that name sound familiar?*

Ares's voice come back. "This is my other wolf, Achilles. This is his pain."

He allows for emotions to run through Wolfe's brain to his nerves; and Wolfe begins to feel anger, guilt, grief, and anguish.

Wolfe looks at the warrior and says commandingly, "Ready our warrior. We take Hector and get our vengeance."

The warrior nods and runs out.

Wolfe grabs his helmet and moves to the battlefield. He sees Trojans not facing him. He runs up and drives his sword into the back of one soldier, then pulls his sword out of him. The other one faces him, and Wolfe quickly slash his neck. He hears Ares again.

"I give you my strength and will."

He begins to feel strength come over him, and it burns. Everything starts to throb as his heart rate increases. He looks, and it feels like he is altering time itself.

He begins to move forward and thinks, *Who are we looking for?*

Ares replies to his thoughts, "Hector."

Wolfe yells, "Hector!"

He sees a well-dressed soldier looks at him and gets the attention of a soldier on horseback. The soldier sees him and turns his horse to try to get away. Wolfe sees a dead body with a spear in him. He rips it out and aims as his vision is throbbing, almost slowing down. He throws the spear at the horse and kills it. The horse falls over, landing on Hector's legs. Wolfe moves up and begins to pick up speed as the guard comes to stop Achilles from exacting revenge.

One the soldiers throws a spear, and Wolfe sees it, and the throbbing lets him move out of the way very quickly. The soldier draws his sword, and Wolfe throws his sword at the soldier. It flies with impossible accuracy, making impact on his neck. The handle sticks out his neck, the blade deep in his throat. The rest of the guards gets Hector off the ground, and he starts to limp away with a broken leg. Wolfe pulls his sword out the soldier's neck and sees Hector trying to limp away. Wolfe moves toward the guard, waiting for him. He runs full sprint, and the first two of the group thrust center mass. Wolfe jumps back, then lunges forward, slicing at their necks, releasing blood as they fall. One of the last three guards thrust his spear at Wolfe's side. He grabs the spear and shoves it by his leg and step on it, making the spear snap. Then he pulls him closer as Wolfe digs his blade into the guard. The last two take off running as they are cowards.

Ares voice comes back. "My father told me to stay out of this war shortly after my sister got involved, then I had to even the odds, but the Trojans disappointed me."

Wolfe looks confused.

Ares says calmly, "Onward."

Wolfe looks up and sees Hector getting close enough for his archers to cover him. Wolfe chases him down and grabs him and flips him toward him, knocking him down in the process.

Wolfe stands over him and says calmly, "Stand up and face your choices, coward."

Hector gets up and screams, "I have no weapon. Who is the real coward?"

Wolfe drops his weapons and tosses them away.

Hector watches Achilles disarm himself and prepares to meet the boatman.

Wolfe walks closer, and Hector throws the first punch. Wolfe catches the punch and snaps his arm, breaking it. Hector falls down, and Wolfe grabs his broken arm, holding him up, then Wolfe stomps on Hector's knees. He hears a snap. Hector takes a deep breath, then cry out in pain.

Wolfe hears Ares again.

"Quit playing with your food."

Wolfe grabs one of his knives off his chest and puts it in Hector's throat and leaves him to choke on his blood. He watches the body go through emotions as it falls still, then he grabs one of the legs and begins to drag him away like a like dead prey. Wolfe feels a claw grab him, and Ares pulls him out of the grave.

Aten and the doctor are watching the vitals, and one of the guests sees crimson coming off Wolfe's fist.

He says, "What is that coming off his hand?"

Everyone looks and are amazed.

Aten looks at the doctor and smiles, knowing that Wolfe is making progress instead of exploding.

Aten says, "Run an energy check on that."

The doctor grabs a remote control car with a several readers on it and sends it in. The car gets close to Wolfe, and it tries to read the energy. The doctor looks at the measurements.

Aten, looking over the shoulder, asks, "What kind of energy is that?"

The doctor says slowly, "It's nothing we discovered yet, like it is not from this universe."

Aten looks at the doctor and replies slowly, "Send in the car."

They send in a remote car that is covered in measuring instruments. It wheels up to Wolfe's hand and starts to read the energy.

The doctor mutters, "That's not possible."

The doctor keeps looking, and the energy comes out from the hand and slaps the car back to where it came from.

The guests look in astonishment.

The doctor says, "Well, that answer my next question."

Aten looks at the doctor and whispers, "What question was that?"

The doctor replies, "Is it just energy, or is a life force?"

Aten looks at the doctor, and the doctor continues, "This could be the proof of God, what makes us different than animals."

Aten looks amazed and says, "I am going to continue monitoring on the other side."

Wolfe ends up back at the graveyard, trying to gather his thoughts and pull himself together. He looks at Ares, then gets up, slowing his breathing.

Ares stares at his warrior as he works through his panic attack and says, "May we continue, or do you need armor to still your feet?"

Wolfe looks at him confused and asks, "What does any of that mean?"

Ares snarls at Wolfe and says, "Does thou have the courage to continue, or should I send you to Taurus for being a disappointment?"

Wolfe looks at Ares, unmoved by Ares, then says, "We shall press on then, you giant Chihuahua."

Ares smiles at the spirit of the insult and walks to the next grave, and it reads Leonidas.

Wolfe gets excited to see the famous gravestone.

Ares stops his hand and says, "My last civilization. I was deemed to hostile for the world, and like leaves in the fall, the empire fell." He puts hand on the stone, and the dirt begins to fall in, and Ares's hand goes to Wolfe's shoulder.

Wolfe turns around and says, "Enough of that. I can get into a grave myself."

Ares unhands him, and Wolfe looks at the grave. Ares uses one hand and pushes him in, smiling with his jackal-like teeth.

Wolfe falls in and lands on a ledge facing a body of water. He sees ships coming and footsteps behind him.

One of them yells, "My king, they are coming to finish us."

Wolfe stands up and looks at the soldier wearing Spartan amor. He looks down and sees his amor.

The soldier sees Wolfe looking at the insignia of his shield and yells, "We shall die for Sparta."

Wolfe begins to hear Ares again, "I loved my Spartan, always ready for the war to come. Get ready, Leonidas. This is a test of courage."

Wolfe sees the soldier running back to formation. Wolfe looks back at the ships and then follows the soldier. He walks to their camp and the soldier start cheering.

"Leonidas."

Ares's voice comes back. "Give them a speech on death and glory, my wolf."

Wolfe looks around and hushes the soldiers, then says, "My men, it has been an honor to serve you, as you have served me."

The soldiers raise their spears.

Wolfe continues, "Today we shall meet death and show him how true warrior go into the dark."

Ares's voice comes back. "You are even enticing me."

The soldiers start pounding the spears at a slow pace.

Wolfe proceeds, "When the rest of our homeland hears of our story, they will not know us as men but as wolves of these hills."

The soldiers stand up and pound faster.

Wolfe picks up his spear and point, yelling, "They can come to kill us, but we shall be forever know as Ares's soldier, and I say we show them what that mean! Men, prepare for death's inky black shadow!"

The soldiers start yelling their battle cries.

Ares's voice comes back. "Now to death."

Wolfe heads out, and he starts to see soldier above him with arrows. He sees a Persian army marching toward them.

Ares grants his vision to Wolfe, and Wolfe sees their heartbeat. They are going fast.

Ares's voice comes back. "They fear you guys. This is what it means to be a warrior, my wolf. Even when the odds are against us, we are still feared."

Wolfe feels a claw grab him and is ripped out of the grave by Ares.

Wolfe looks around the graveyard and finally asks, "What is the point of this?"

Ares moves closer and looks at the sunset and say calmly, "The truth?"

Wolfe looks at Ares, then proceeds to say, "Yes."

Ares responds, "It's been awhile since I walked the earth and needed someone to talk of my warrior blood."

Wolfe looks at him, disappointed in the answer, then says, "So I was your therapy."

Ares snarls and says, "Not exactly. I was checking to see if my bloodline held true."

Wolfe looks at Ares.

Ares turns to Wolfe, then says, "A lot of you will believe you to be crazy. However, our truth is our truth, and you have observed it from the beginning."

Wolfe thinks of everyone who thought he was crazy and dismissed him.

Ares continues, "I know. That's why you were so self-destructive. I am here to offer relief and proof, my wolf."

Wolfe gets teary eyed as he remembers all the pain and says, "I just never had a chance, did I?"

Ares looks at Wolfe with sympathy and says solemnly, "No, you didn't, but I can rectify that now." Ares takes his claw and turns Wolfe back to Valhalla and says, "This is where we belong, all the warrior and even your mentors."

Wolfe looks and sees his sergeant walking around, drinking and talking with the warrior of the past, and he looks around more and sees his father.

Ares sighs and says, "It's not technically heaven, but it a good place where warriors can be warrior."

Wolfe looks at his paradise and says, "Why is it not heaven?"

Ares smiles and responds, "Heaven is for the peaceful. Do you know what happens when warriors go to heaven?"

Wolfe smiles and says, "I can see how that can be a problem."

Ares kneels and gets to Wolf's eye level, then asks, "So what is your choice? Come to Valhalla or go back home to them." Ares plays a live stream in his eyes of what Wolfe can see from his physical eyes, and Wolfe can see everyone watching as an experiment.

Wolfe responds, "I choose Valhalla, Ares."

Ares stands up and responds, "Good, because they wait for you."

Wolfe sees people from his past wave at him, and Wolfe tears up, finally happy and found a place of belonging.

Ares sighs and says, "Officium vitae," and then he walks away.

7

Aten and the doctor watch Wolfe's vitals. The honored guests begin to get restless, and the senator finally asks, "How long is this going to take, Director?"

The director thinks of the past test subject and gets annoyed and replies, "Do you know how many people we have lost?"

The senator snaps, "Clearly not enough."

Aten stares at the senator in disgust, and the doctor yells, "No!"

Aten turns around and sees Wolfe's pulse die down to a flatline.

The honored guests begin to get up.

The doctor wonders why Wolfe didn't explode.

The guests open the door.

Wolfe's pulse comes back, and the guests turn around to see Wolfe's body moving and breathing.

Aten yells, "You glorious bastard."

Wolfe moves his hand, and everyone starts clapping. Wolfe looks up with crimson eyes, then rips the restraint cables around him. Aten sees Wolfe rip the cables and smiles. It is complete. Those cables are strong enough to hold a full-grown elephant for days, and a human just ripped it out of the ground.

Aten turns around and gets on the intercom, then says, excited, "Stand by, Wolfe."

Wolfe's body rips the rest of the cords out of the ground.

The senator looks in amazement and says, "Oh, countries will pay big money for him."

Wolfe's body gets up and looks at the window and sees heartbeats. He walks to the window and puts his hands on the window, seeing the living organisms in the room. He waits to see what their plan is.

One of the guests asks, "Can he see us, because I don't like his stare?"

Aten looks at Wolfe's golden eyes and says, "This is two-way mirror and made of bulletproof glass. There is no way he can hear us or see us."

The senator stands up and says, "How much, Director?"

Wolfe's eyes watch him and sees the auction about to take place. Wolfe takes his hand and flicks the glass, causing it to shatter. The guests stare in horror as Wolfe's body climbs in the window. Security moves in and aims their weapons at Wolfe's body.

Wolfe's body finally says in a stoic deep tone, "Those will only anger me. I plead for thou safety."

Aten looks at Wolfe and says, "Stand down, Wolfe."

Wolfe's eyes meet Aten, and they search his soul and then stops. "You are honest, so I shall be honest. I am not Wolfe." Wolfe continues, "I am Ares, the angel of war. However, you shall call me Violence till further notice."

The senator takes a seat and says, "You are government property."

Violence looks at the senator and sees greed, bribes, innocent blood, drugs, and other corruption. Violence walks closer to the senator, and the guards start to scream commands.

"Halt!"

One of them shoots, and the bullet hits Violence's head. It doesn't even make a dent in his skin. Violence looks at the guard, who is now scared, and looks back the senator.

Violence kicks a leg of his chair, making him fall down, and Violence growls. "I have seen though sins, and you have been weighed, and death is your punishment." Violence summons his kopis out of his hand and puts it to the senator's chest. The senator pisses himself in fear. Violence looks and is disgusted. He says, "I hate a coward. You have sent others to their death for money, but you will not take you fair share?"

Aten steps in and says, "What will we need to make this peaceful?"

Violence says, "An island, his island in particular."

The senator responds, stuttering, "I...I...don't have an...is—"

Violence stops him and says, "Even when almost dead, does thou still choose to tell lies?"

The senator looks at Violence and says frantically, "Fine, it is yours, just don't come near me again."

Violence replies, "There are no pacts between wolves and lambs."

Senator pleads, scared, "Please!"

Violence lets him go and says, growling, "I will let you go, but know that the ones you sent to their death wait for you in the afterlife to have their own fun." Violence smiles and laughs menacingly.

The senator crawls away, and Violence throws his sword in the wall next to him. The senator pauses to look at the sword and sees it throbbing in the wall, almost like it is crying for blood.

Violence says, "I expect the island and its slave released by the week's end."

The senator nods and goes away.

The rest of the group tries to escape the room. Violence stares at them, reading them as they try to slink away. Violence turns around and allows them to leave as he pulls a chair and calls, "Aten and Doctor!"

Aten and the doctor look at Violence as he takes a seat and points at two more chairs. They cautiously take a seat, and Violence begins a conversation, stating, "I do apologize for my introduction. However, I was in need to make a statement."

Aten speaks up, saying, "So you had to ruin what was supposed to be a huge discovery."

Violence looks at Aten in anger and says, "Those people were horrible souls. The reason why you are in my presence is because of you, Aten. By the way, a very strong name."

Aten looks at Violence, confused.

Violence continues, "We can be partners as long as our goal meets together. I could take the earth by storm, but it will not suffice."

Aten looks at the doctor, then back at Violence. "What are you proposing?"

Violence relaxes and states, "I can help in your endeavors if you will help me in mine. I know you are chasing a new weapon, hence why I am here, and I know who the enemy are, but the island is mine, and they are never to be used."

Aten looks at the doctor, and the doctor is astonished as he says, "How do you know about what we are planning?"

Violence looks the doctor in the eyes and says, "I can see your very soul, every dirty thing you know."

The doctor gulps, and Aten speaks up. "That is just one of our projects. What about the others?"

Violence stares and says, "I will put the other countries in line as well. You might have world peace for once."

Aten looks at Violence in a negative stare, and Violence chuckles.

"We all know you cannot maintain peace. However, I will make sure you enemies stay in line."

Aten looks at the doctor and says, "We have a bargain?"

Violence summons his spear, then grips its head and slices his hand, then holds its out. Aten looks at Violence in disgust. He take Violence's hand as the blood goes around. Aten's hand is burning but is not harmed.

Aten quickly states, "What was that?"

Violence says, "A pact to make sure you hold your word. If not, I will see you in the afterlife, unless God supersedes me."

Aten looks at Violence glowing eyes and says, "I believe. However, I am not scared of what's is in the afterlife."

Violence stares into Aten's eyes and sees Aten leading the charge against enemy fire, him standing by a deathbed of a dying soldier and his grief for the mask consuming lives.

Violence says, "I trust you, Aten. I have seen your life and you were honorable. Some of your soldiers are in Valhalla."

Aten looks at him with doubt, and Violence says, "Gabriel Martinez, 128 engineer company."

Aten's eyes begin water, and Violence says, "Do not feel grief. He died a warrior and is now living a warrior's dream."

Aten nods his head and says, "Thank you."

Violence looks around and gets up. He states, "I need to shower and plan. Meanwhile, I suggest you start finding our next objection."

Violence heads out, and Aten looks at the cameras and sees the esteemed guests evacuating.

The doctor says, "I would leave too."

Aten gets on the radio and says, "No one is permitted to leave. Anyone who takes off will be shot down. Please report back to conference room A."

The doctor looks at Aten and says, "Why are you making them stay?"

Aten replies, "If we are going to do what Violence needs, then we need more support, financial and military support."

The doctor nods his head and arms the anti-aircraft and put the guards on alert.

Aten says, "Let's get to the conference room."

Aten and the doctor show up to the conference room, and the esteemed guests are escorted to the room, where they are pointed at a seat by gunpoint. They take their seat, and one of the guests yells, "What is the purpose of this? Why are we being held hostage?"

The guests keep murmuring among each other.

Aten does a head count and sees one is missing. The door opens, and the senator is being carried in by several guards and is restrained to a chair. The senator looks at Aten in disgust.

Aten states, "I am sorry for doing this in this manner. However, I need to debrief you on what has happened and start planning for the future."

The senator looks at his restraints, and one of the guests says, "We will not work with a monster of that degree. No one can bargain with that snake."

Violence walks in the room in tactical black gear with his right sleeved torn off and takes a seat next to Aten.

The senator gets green at the sight of his bully.

Aten nods at Violence, then states, "We have come to an agreement, and we are here now to talk about the future."

The guests see that Violence is calm and begin to calm down. One of the guests speaks up.

"We, me and the people of Argentina, are hoping of handling a private military operation. Is that something you can help with, Violence?"

Violence looks at the guest with his gold eyes and sees his soul and nods. He replies, "If the senator holds his bargain, I will hold mine."

The guest looks at Violence and says, "Then I shall send the details to your superiors."

Violence gives him a death glare, and the guest gulps and says, "Or your partners? Sorry, I meant no disrespect."

Violence replies, "Some taken. However, this is business, so we shall proceed but thou shall not make it a habit."

The guest nods, and the senator raises his concern.

"Why should you concern yourself with Argentina?"

Violence looks at the senator, then says, "Because the private military group is acting in bad faith, raping and killing innocents."

The senator replies, "Those are just rumors."

The guest replies, "I have seen them do it."

Violence raises his voice and says, "I know they are, and I will handle it."

The senator states, "Why am I the only one paying the price?"

Violence looks at the senator and says, "Because your acts have been inhumane, and if you would like me to spill those secrets, continues pressing the Wolfe."

The senator gets bold and says, "I have no secrets."

Violence smiles, then says, "Right, that's why the private military group in Argentina is taking women and children to the very island promised to me and why same soldiers are being paid rather handsomely by a funds of the less fortunate to make some of your sick entertainment parties."

The guests looks at the senator, and Aten lowers his head.

The senator lowers his head and says, "That is their will."

Violence replies, "And this is mine."

Aten gets control. "That is the beginning of it. We shall be in touch. You are now allowed to leave in peace."

The guards cut the guests loose, including the senator, and the group waits for the guest to leave.

—◊◊—

Hawke is sitting at her desk and starts to think about Wolfe and if the director held his word. She gets up and checks her email and sees a new message from a military email. She opens it, and it reads, "Hello,

I am a therapist at Fort Leavenworth. I would just like you know that Wolfe has been getting your mail. However, he is refusing to respond for the reason, and I quote, 'Why, so she can give me more shit.' If you would like more information, please contact me." She reads down and sees his number and name.

She picks up her phone and calls the number right away, and she finally reaches the therapist.

The therapist says, "Hello, thank you for calling. How may I help you?"

Hawke responds, "Hi, yes, I am calling about Wolfe."

There is a long silence, and he says, "Yes, Wolfe, of course."

Hawke looks at the phone, confused, then proceeds. "How is my soldier doing?"

The therapist has a longer pause, and he finally says, "He is rehabilitating very well."

Hawke hears a female voice say, "He is lying, press him."

Hawke replies, "Well, I would like to talk to him."

The therapist says, "Well, that's not in my range to make happen."

Hawke replies aggressively, "Look, Doctor, I know you are lying. Where is he?"

She hears therapist takes a deep breath and says, "This stays between me and you?"

Hawke replies, "Of course. Now tell me."

The therapist replies, "There is black site in North Dakota. Some high-ranking man took him for an experiment."

Hawke replies, "And you didn't see anything wrong with it?"

The therapist retorts, "It wasn't my choice."

Hawke leans back and breathes deeply. "Thank you for you what you have given me."

Therapist pauses and then says, "Of course. Is there anything I can help you with?"

Hawke replies, "Not at this moment, no."

Hawke hangs up the phone and Googles North Dakota and sees a story about how a senator almost died in a helicopter crash. Hawke sighs and begins filling out paperwork for a leave of absence.

Atlas first comes out of a ground, and he slowly pulls himself up and makes room for Cyclops. They look at the city of Hollywood.

Cyclops sees the sun and takes a deep breath, then coughs. Cyclops states, "It stinks here. What happened?"

Atlas looks at his old friend and replies, "Humans—a mistake that I will soon rectify, my old friend."

They hear a honk behind them from a wealthy individual driving a nice car. Atlas gives the car a death stare, then Cyclops goes over to the car to investigate.

The owner gets out in awe and says, "Are y'all stupid? The movie sets are over there."

Cyclops looks at the driver and replies kindly, "Why would you say that, my little friend?" Cyclops is towering over the driver.

The driver states, "Hey, dumb asses, get out of the road, you retards."

Cyclops picks up the human.

He starts to scream for help. "Help me!"

Cyclops eats the human and kicks the car down the mountain.

Atlas smiles at Cyclops's initial reaction. Atlas walks to him and says, "We need to move. I am going to put you in the sand and sun. I need you to find a certain object for me."

Cyclops looks like he is sick, and Atlas sees it and asks, "What is wrong?"

Cyclops replies nauseously, "He tasted nasty."

Atlas smiles and replies, "They don't eat from the earth anymore. They are all sick, and we are their remedy. Do you understand me?"

Cyclops nods, and Atlas makes a dark circle, and Cyclops walks through to the Sahara Desert. He touches the ground, and a dark purple pulses, and he makes another circle and goes to Greece.

—∭—

The next day comes, and Aten is in the conference room looking at Venezuela and the commander of the mercenaries.

Violence walks in with a black cup of coffee and says, "What are we looking at?"

Aten answers, "These are the mercenaries we need to neutralize to start holding up our deal."

Violence looks at them and growls, then takes a seat as the doctor walks in with the paperwork.

The doctor looks at the screen and sees the group and the location, then says, "Well, that was fast."

Aten replies, "I have been watching. Apparently, the senator tipped them off, and they are mobilizing."

Violence scoffs, "It won't make a difference."

Aten looks at Violence and replies, "It won't. We will have transport ETA 1 hour, so gear up."

Violence looks at Aten and says, "This is all I need," as he puts his hands out.

Aten smiles. "My apologies. I forgot, your code name for commutations will be Hellhound 4."

Violence looks confused and then asks, "Communications and hellhounds are weak."

Aten looks confused to now, and he tries to back it up. "No, it is a code name."

Violence is even more confused. "That is not my name. My name is already a code name."

Violence lets it go and heads back to his room to wait for the green light. He lies on his bed and feels his chest where his wedding ring is and tenderly touches it and thinks of Aphrodite. His eyes begin to glow more and more with the thought of her, and eventually, a small tear comes out of Violence. He feels his face and touches the tear. He looks at it and grunts.

8

The next day arrives, and Violence sits in his room reminiscing about his life before he fell as he plays with the ring. He hears a knock at the door, and he growls, "What?"

A soldier replies, "You are being requested in the conference room."

Violence looks annoyed but gets up and complies. He walks out his room to the conference room at a fast pace. He walks in and sees a screen with several armed guards holding a briefcase wearing the mercenary's logo on a patch.

Violence stares, and Aten says, "They have been on the move for a while, but they moved their gear and all of other assets by train. However, this briefcase has been with higher-ups."

Violence continues to stare at the screen, then says, "Acquire the briefcase."

Aten nods and continues, "We have a feeling if the senator is going to retaliate, it will be with them."

Violence smiles and says, "Let's castrate this pedophile."

Aten looks at the doctor, and the doctor flips some switches and says, "Transport will be ready in an hour."

Violence looks at the doctor and says, "You depress me," then walks away to the landing strip.

The doctor looks at Aten, and Aten looks back and says, "I've gotten used to it."

The doctor looks at his desk and sees Violence's earpiece and runs after him.

Violence reaches the landing strip and sees a plane fueling up.

The doctor reaches him in time and try to talk but is out of breath "You…you fo…"

Violence looks at the doctor disgusted at his cardio shape, then says, "For the love of everything holy, when was the last time you got any cardio in your workout?"

The doctor, still trying to catch his breath, says, "Last…year."

Violence looks at the doctor and says, "Well, why did you run after like a child chasing a chicken?"

The doctor catches his breath and looks at Violence weirdly, then says, "I don't comprehend that. However, here is your communication piece," and hands a case to Violence.

Violence takes it, and the doctor gets word from Aten.

"Show him the armory and let him take what he needs and report back to what he took."

The doctor replies, "Copy that." He looks at Violence, then signals for Violence to follow.

Violence looks at the doctor in confusion.

The doctor says, "Will you please follow me? I will show you our armory."

Violence follows the doctor to a room filled with weapons and body armor. Violence looks around and sees two knives. He grabs them, then leaves the room.

The doctor, confused on why he didn't take anything else, shouts to him, "Do you need anything else?"

Violence replies, "No, this will do."

The doctor reports back to Aten, "Two Ka-Bars."

He hears back from Aten, "That's all?"

The doctor replies, "Yes."

Aten retorts, "He is going to take on a platoon with two knives?"

The doctor looks at the nearest camera and shrugs at the question.

Violence reaches his position as he overlooks the slums and sees one full building. He begins to move, and he hears Aten in his earpiece.

"We are tracking the convoy. They are several hundred clicks out. We are still trying to determine the destination."

Violence stays stern and replies, "Have we considered the only building that has armed guards, fencing, and looks like military vehicles?"

There is a long pause, and the doctor finally replies, "We have not considered, but that is probably a good start."

Violence begins to move. He puts on his amber sunglasses and moves to a bar across the street. The guards see him walk into the bar and think nothing of it. Violence takes a seat and a young boy walks over to him holding a portable fan. The kid looks at Violence, and his father comes and tells the kid, "Go play in the other room."

Violence stares at the kid, reading his innocent soul, and sees his father being beaten by the guard as he hides. Violence looks at the father and sees he is bruised.

The man says, "Please, we don't want any more problems."

Violence says in a calm voice, "I am not one of those animals."

The man looks confused, then proceeds to ask, "What would you like to drink?"

Violence responds, "Beer, please."

The man nods and goes to refrigerator and grabs a Venezuelan beer and brings it back to him.

Violence takes his glasses off, and the man sees Violence's crimson eyes and is stuck looking.

Violence, feeling the heavy stare, asks, "Is there a problem?"

The man says, "What are you?"

Violence smiles and says, "I am the angel of war."

The man looks away, and Violence stops him by asking him, "What did they take from you?"

The man looks at Violence, broken, and replies sheepishly, "My wife, my daughter, and my pride."

Violence feels his ring and asks back, "Are they in there?"

The man looks at the building. Scared of being caught, he gives a quick glance and says, "That is where they took them."

Violence smiles and replies, "They shall be with you soon."

He hears Aten on the communication, "Don't give your position away yet."

Violence waves off the man, and the man goes back to his son. Violence talks back to Aten, "Did you hear that?"

There is a long pause, and Aten finally responds, "I did, and it is unfortunate."

Violence responds, "It is for them."

Aten responds, "Hang tight. They are coming, Hellhound 4."

Violence relaxes and replies, "I am Violence, and I will do as I see fit." Violence takes his earpiece out and waits.

A convoy of black Tahoes drive up to the building, and Violence watches them get out of their vehicles. Several guards are decked out in black private-section gear. Violence watches them file out and set up a parameter. One them looks at Violence drinking his beer, and the guard continues on the mission.

A guy in a suit gets out with a briefcase handcuffed to his right arm, and four more guards armed to the teeth get out with him and begin to escort the VIP into the building.

Violence stands up and begins to make his way to the guards.

One of the guards approaches Violence and commands, "Halt."

Violence stops and stares at the guard, and the guard points back to the bar.

Violence looks at the guard and says, "Return that item, and you can keep the rest." He points to the guy's briefcase.

The guard yells, "Turn away," and readies his weapon.

Violence looks at the guard and sees everyone now has their eyes on him. The rest of the guards comes to investigate as the VIP stares at Violence, confused.

The guard sees the other guards and begins to get more aggressive and yells, "Down on the ground!"

Violence looks at the ground and says quietly, "Why would I go back to where I just came from?"

Violence's hands begin to turn a golden crimson, and he summons his shield and kopis and readies for combat.

The guards open fire, and the shield stops all the bullets. Violence puts his hand on the ground and sees their heartbeats as their heart rate spike. Confused, he smells the air, and he can smell a sweet caramel. He breathes in again, loving the smell of fear. The guards begin to maneuver, and Violence snaps out of his euphoric states and rushes on one and slices his arm and cuts his throat. He turns to face the other guard as they reloaded and begins to empty mags into the shield again. Violence puts his kopis down and summons a chain and waits till he hears a reload, then he whips the chain, striking most of them. The chain rips through parts of their bodies like a chainsaw. The man in suit begins to run to the building, and the remaining mercenaries guarding the VIP throw tear gas at Violence to try to subdue him. Violence takes a deep breath of it, and mercenaries look at him in shock. The mercenaries begin to unload on Violence again and maneuver much quicker than the other guards. Violence throw his shield at one of them, knocking him down, and throws his chain at another. The chain gets stuck in the mercenary's body armor, and Violence yanks it, forcing him to come closer. As Violence looks in the eyes of the mercenary, he can see all the ugly sins of war he has committed. The mercenary is stunned as he stares, reliving those memories in Violence's eyes. Violence punches his chest and rips out his heart, then drops the body. The rest of the mercenaries move out of the building and take positions and take aim. Violence begins to swing his chain and throw the chain in one of their faces. The chain rips through the face of the mercenary, and the last two mercenaries begin to run away. Violence holds his hand out, and a spear appears in his hand, and he throws the spear, striking one of them in the back. The spear hits, making several different breaking sounds as it impales him. He falls on his knees and sees the spear head coming through his chest as he slowly dies. Violence turns and whips one of the mercenary, breaking his amor as he stands still, trying to move away. Violence walks to him and kicks the back of knee and snaps his neck. He admires his work and looks back at the building. He holds out his hands and out grows a golden crimson, and his weapon disappears into the ground.

He walks to the building, and he puts his hand on the building and sees one heart. It is beating with fear and sees the heart going upstairs. He takes his hand off the building and grabs the two knives he took from the base and begins climbing the building with the knives, digging one knife in after another as he scales the wall. He puts his hand on the wall and sees three heartbeats going berserk on the top floor, and then they stop. Violence takes his hand off the wall and continues scaling the building till he hits the top floor and finds a window. He breaks them, then enters the room. Violence looks around and sees a vaulted door that is locked. Violence walks to the room and puts his hand on the door and sees three heartbeats both consumed by fear. Violence puts his knifes away and starts punching the door, a crimson blast leaving his fist with each hit. The door begins to dent with each hit.

The VIP begins to look around for weapons but can't find anything but a pencil and gold. Then he looks at the briefcase and begins to open it.

Another hard punch hits the door, and the metal begins to buckle more and more.

The VIP finally opens the briefcase and sees a red rose mask with two spears on the right cheek.

Another hard hit from Violence, and metal begins to bend inward.

The VIP takes the mask and puts it on as Violence fist finally reach through the door and begins to pull the door open. Violence gets the door open and sees the VIP burning from the inside out. He stands in shock and confused as the flame inside fully consumes him and he is burned to a skeleton and ashes begin to fly off. Violence reaches down and grabs the mask and looks at it and begins to feel his chest where the ring is. He hears a whimper and shushing. He looks over to the noises and sees a woman and a kid tied up in a corner. He looks at them and pulls his knife. The mask emits a flame that goes up Violence's arm. He growls in pain.

"I was not going to hurt them."

He looks at the mask. He takes the knife and cuts the woman loose; and the mother, seeing Violence's eyes, immediately start praying for safety. Violence tries to cut the kid free, but the mother tries to interrupt Violence. Violence pushes her away as he cuts the kid free. The kid, seeing Violence's eyes, is not afraid of him and goes to hug him. The mother sits there shocked and scared for the kid's safety. Violence is confused by the hug as his eyes become a little bit more gold color than crimson. The mask burns his hand again, and Violence embraces the little girl back as the little girl says, "I knew God would send an angel to free us."

Violence lets go and points the mother as the kid runs to the mom. The mom grabs her and gets up. Violence signals the woman to wait as he goes and grabs the gold and hands it to the mother. She takes it sheepishly as Violence tell her quietly, "Rebuild this land with this, and do not be greedy, or I shall see your land again."

The mother nods and says, "Thank you."

They begin to walk out. They reach the front door, and people are gathered around. Some are looting the body of the guards, but the father sees his wife and daughter and runs to them, crying. Violence watches for a moment as his eyes becomes gold. The mask begins to be soothing warm, and his eyes go back to crimson as he walks away and calls for an evac.

"Hellhound 4 to Command."

Aten answers, "Command here. We read you loud and clear."

Violence looks at the mask, then says, "I need an evacuation, and we need to have words, humans."

Aten responds, "Roger that. Evacuation en route."

Violence climbs a mountain and waits for the evac to show up. He stares at the mask and begins remembering the memories of Aphrodite and his downfall as an angel.

He mutters to the mask, "You know this was my plan to see you again, but it was not supposed to be like this." Violence looks at the mask and chuckles a little. "This reminds of the first time I lost you to the craftsman, who would figure I would get a second chance to do it again."

The mask begins to heat up, and Violence sets it down on the ground as he grunts, "Do not lose your temper."

The mask catches a small blaze in the grass surrounding the mask.

Violence smiles and says, "Soon you will have your chance to get revenge, but for now shall, we just enjoy each other's company."

The mask simmers down, and the fire goes away as Violence sees a black Hawk coming to get him. He grabs the mask and waits for the helicopter to land.

9

The helicopter lands back at base, and Violence doesn't even wait for it to land. He gets off the helicopter holding the mask in his hand and begins to walk to the hanger where he sees the doctor. Violence walks close enough and yells, "Where is he?"

The doctor, surprised by his sheer aggression, fumbles his words. "Who...what are you talking about?"

Violence closes the gap and yells in the doctor face. "Where is Aten!"

The doctor point inside the base.

Violence looks at the petrified doctor and grabs his shirt and drags him, then throws him in the general direction. The doctor walks with a purpose, scared of Violence. Violence looks around outside and can sense he is being watched.

In the fields of the base, she lies prone in a ghillie suit, watching every move as she thinks, *What have you done now Wolfe?*

She keeps watching as she sees Wolfe's body looks directly at her scope as he mutters, "Athena, you have sent your own, have you?"

Hawke breaks her sight picture as she hears a female voice.

"We need to get in there."

Hawke looks around, unsure what she just hears. As she looks back, she sees Wolfe walking away. The doctor leads him inside to Aten.

Violence walks away as he turns to follow the doctor. The doctor walks into the conference room followed by Violence. Violence throws the mask on the table and stares at Aten with malicious intent, then says, "When were you going to tell me?"

Aten looks confused and replies, "Tell you what."

Violence scoffs at the ignorance, and he growls, "When were you going to tell me that they are more angelic relic on this planet of dirt."

Aten looks at the mask, then replies, "We didn't know. We had suspected something, but we did not know what it was."

Violence stares in Aten's eyes, searching his memory, and finds he is telling the truth.

Aten feels a cold shiver go down his spine as Violence searches for his answer.

Violence calms down and takes a seat. "Well, there is the prize."

Aten looks at the metal mask in the light. The mask mirrors a rainbow. Aten finishes observing it and says, "Do you know how to activate it?"

Violence scoffs again, almost annoyed. "I do. However, we shall leave her in this form for now."

Aten looks confused, then looks at the doctor, still shaken up by Violence's aggression. He sighs and says, "Why should we leave...her?"

Violence looks down at his ring, and Aten follows his gaze, and then says, "She was someone to you, wasn't she?"

Violence snaps out of it and growls, "She is the one that killed who I was."

Aten takes a seat and sighs. "I am sorry truly."

Violence growls, "I do not need your sympathy, human."

Aten slides the mask back to Violence, and Violence touches it gently, then it ignites in a flame. Violence picks it up and says in a defeated voice, "Calm down."

The mask ignites even hotter in Violence's hand.

He growls, "Fine, then you can stay outside where you cannot burn anything." He sighs aggressively and walks out with the mask.

Then Aten chimes, "Leave it on the table."

Violence slowly turns, aghast. He is stunned that he is taking orders form a human, as the mask burns hotter, searing his skin. Violence throws the mask on the table, and the flames extinguish as it hits the table. Violence looks at it and finally accepts what he has to do.

Violence states, "Bring me a list of people who are available for a similar process to Wolfe."

Aten nods and looks at the doctor with approval.

The doctor gets up and goes over to a thick file and brings it to the table. The doctor looks through it to check it, then hands it over to Violence.

Violence begins looking through, tossing profile after profile out.

Aten and the doctor watch him go through the file, tossing out paper after paper, eventually Aten says, "Any specific reason why those people will work."

Violence responds, "They will not suffice due to them being male."

The doctor looks at Violence, then says, "Why does the subject have to be female?"

Violence responds, "Because Aphrodite is a woman, not a man. As much as she wants to be, it may be difficult to try and put her in a male body. She will kill him before she accepts him."

The doctor looks at Violence and says, "Aphrodite?"

Violence continues focusing on profiles and responds, "Yes, the harlot. She is not as nice as you would assume."

The doctor gulps at the thought of carnage of more people.

Violence finally looks at one profile and reads everything, then hands it to Aten. Violence says, "This is our woman. Ashley Raine."

Aten looks at her profile and sees a small woman at the age of nineteen with several murder charges. He gives it to the doctor and looks at Violence and says, "What is so special about her?"

Violence responds, "Look at the murders. They were out of rage and passion. That is her attitude in a nutshell."

The mask begins to get hot again, and Violence quickly says, "I am only playing a practical joke."

The mask remains hot but begins to simmer down.

Aten looks at Violence, then says, "Is the mask a living being?"

Violence responds, "It is our essence. Think of it like our soul."

Aten retorts, "Why did your mask not doing anything when we talked to it."

Violence smiles and responds, "Because you are no one of note. We can hear through the mask when other angels are talking to other angels."

Aten shrugs and tries to take the mask of the table but burns himself.

"Son of a bitch," he yelps as he pulls his hand back.

Violence giggles and grabs the mask, then pulls his knife and balances it on the knife.

"Where are we going?"

Aten responds, "To the chamber where we summoned you."

Violence nods and moves to the room while balancing the mask. He sets the mask on the table, and they leave the room.

Violence looks at her mask, and then Aten says, "We will need time to get this girl here."

Violence rubs his ring on his chest and nods.

Aten can see Violence is nervous, which makes Aten nervous as well. Aten bites the bullet and asks, "Why are you nervous?"

Violence stops his actions and responds, "My mistakes are my own," as he leaves.

Violence makes his way to the recreation room and turn the TV on. The news is showing a sighting of a giant around Greece area. Violence looks at the footage and tries to make sense of it all. The doctor barges in. Violence quickly turns around and see the doctor trying to talk through catching his breath.

"Violence, you are...requested in the conference room."

Violence looks back at the TV, and they are talking about weather now. Violence makes his way to the room and sees Aten on a phone call with other generals on the speaker.

He overhears, "Is this your doing, Director? We know you had success with your program."

Aten responds quickly, "I can assure this is not our doing." Aten turns around and sees Violence walking over.

Violence appears before them, eyes crimson red, as the general from Greece says, "Who is speaking in the background?"

Violence scoffs and replies, "I do not have time for introduction again."

Aten retorts, "This is Violence, the fruits of our research."

101

The general replies, "I do not have time for this. Can we get back to topic at hand?"

Violence says, "What is the topic?"

The general responds, "We have a giant in Greece. We have tried communication and reasoning to no avail."

Violence sighs and responds, "Show me pictures of it."

The general puts up several different surveillance photos showing Atlas ripping cars and people apart. Violence looks like he has just seen a ghost and stammers his words.

"There is no way in hell."

The general, quickly looking for answers, replies, "What is it?"

Violence responds, "A Titan."

There is a long silence due to confusion on both sides.

Violence finally breaks his silence and continues, "They were imprisoned in hell."

The general sarcastically says, "Apparently not anymore."

Violence looks disgusted and says, "There is nothing a mortal can do. Stand down and let him roam. I will be there shortly."

The general responds in anger, "There are people getting slaughtered, and you want us to stand down."

Violence eyes stare at the phone and snaps at him. "I am Ares, the angel of war and blood, and I can tell you that if you want to sacrifice your soldiers, keep doing what you're doing. It makes no difference to me."

The general remains quiet, and a voice is heard on a radio telling men to stand down and retreat.

Violence says, "I will be there was quick as I can, but I feel like I will be outmatched. The only thing that can kill a god is another god."

Aten looks at Violence and replies, "We could get the next mask going before you go."

Violence looks at him in questioning notion, and Aten continues, "You are no good to anyone if you are dead."

Violence takes a second and reluctantly agrees.

—◊◊◊—

A day goes by, and Violence hears a bunch of cars driving up. He gets up and puts on easy clothes, then proceeds to walk to the cafeteria. Violence sees Aten and the doctor grabbing coffee.

As they see Violence, they wave him over and say, "Violence, you're up just in time. The subject just got in from Florida."

Violence looks around and asks, "Where is she?"

The doctor replies, "She is being prepped as of right now."

Violence thinks and replies, "That does not answer my question."

Aten responds, "She is in the changing cell where we brought Wolfe."

Violence drops the conversation and heads to the room. As he walks in, he sees her glaring at him in malicious intent.

Violence walks closer, and she says, "What do you want?"

Violence remains quiet, and she continues, "Another strong male here to make a female feel so weak and powerless."

Violence continues to stare, reading her soul.

She can't stop staring at Violence's eyes. She says again, "What do you want?"

Violence finally breaks the silence and replies, "What I want makes no difference. I can only tell you. You are about to meet an angel, and she is very...how do I say this...important to me."

She replies, "And why would I care?"

Violence smirks at the attitude and retorts calmly, "She will offer you something you want."

She scoffs and laughs. "I want nothing from this world."

Violence says calmly, "Good, because what she is offering is not of this world." Violence gets up and begins walking away.

She quickly says to him, "What are you?"

Violence turns around and replies, "A fallen angel," then continues to walk away to Aten and the doctor.

The doctor is watching, and Aten says, "What did you do?"

Violence replies, "Got her ready. Bring in the mask."

The doctor looks at Aten, and Aten nods to the doctor as he pushes a button. Guards come out with the mask and set it in front of her.

She looks and says, "What, are we playing dress-up?"

Aten pushes the intercom and says, "Please put the mask on."

She begrudgingly puts the mask on, and her veins begin to glow with the color of magma. She goes into a coma-like state, the same as with Ares. She wakes up and sees one of her favorite comics that she used to enjoy when she was in high school. She begins to flip through, bringing up old memories, some good some bad. She hears a lovely lady's voice.

"Your soul is very beautiful."

Ashely looks around, unsure of what's going on. She dismisses it and looks around, seeing an old classmates from her high school that followed her to college. A sense of dread follows the realization.

The voice comes back. "Why the feeling?"

Ashely mutters, "This place is not a nice one." Ashely looks around and sees her bully berating a guy.

The voice comes back. "What is her problem?"

Ashely looks down in shames and says, "I made out with her man at a party. We were both drunk."

There is a pause, then the voice come back. "Is that it?"

Ashely looks confused.

The voice continues, "There is no reason to act like that, especially over a man."

Ashely smiles, then says quietly, "Agreed."

The bully sees her staring at them, and she begins to walk over with her friends. Ashely begins packing up her backpack, trying to leave, but the bully has already made her way to the table and slams the table.

Ashley freezes.

The bully says, "What are you looking at, you whore."

Ashely is paralyzed, unable to move.

The bully grabs a carton of milk and pours it over her head. The bully laughs.

The voice comes back. "What are you going to do?"

Ashley's temperature raises and does nothing.

The bully continues to berate her as well.

The voice slowly says in anger, "Burn her."

Ashely looks up at the bully and stands up, then looks at her with pain in her eyes.

The bully sees her stand up and takes it as disrespect and walks over to her and slaps her. She says, "Is this what you wanted, huh, bitch?"

Ashley snaps and quickly punches her in the chest, knocking the wind out of her. Her friends get involved, and she breaks them down one by one. The bully catches her breath and pushes her. Ashely grabs the bully's hair and put one of her hand on her throat.

The voice says, "I'll handle this one."

Her hand begins to burn, and the bully's skin begins to burn off piece by piece as they turn to ashes. The bully tries to get away, yelling and squealing in agony, till she is just a skull in Ashley's hand.

The voice comes back. "Now crush the skull. We deserve worship, and this will serve as a lesson for the rest of the moronic students. Make one an example, and you teach a thousand."

Ashely feels the skull and begins to feel remorse, but it quickly turn to anger when she remembers who it was. She slams it on the ground, shattering it.

The voice comes back. "To the next one now. Sorry, but there is someone I would kill for to see again."

Ashley blinks and is now in an apartment.

The voice comes back. "Where are we now?"

Ashely looks and says, "Me and my ex's apartment. He wasn't a very good man."

The voice comes back. "They hardly ever are. Even the ones who you love the most, they are the ones that do the most damage."

Ashley looks confused and asks, "Have you ever been in love?"

The voice gets quiet and says, "Let's focus on the subject at hand."

Ashely hears an alarm go off. She thinks and starts to panic as she says, "Oh my god, he is almost home, and I need to have dinner ready."

She quickly makes her way to the kitchen and sees nothing is even ready. The door begins to open; and a tall, muscular guy walks in and slips off his boots, then makes his way into the cold kitchen.

He sighs and asks, "Where's dinner?"

Ashley stammers, "Time just g-g-got away from me."

The guy gets annoyed with the answer and yells, "I worked thirteen hours, and the only thing I ask is for you have dinner ready."

Ashley screams back, "I'll have it ready in thirty."

The guys looks at her with malicious intent and moves to her. She tries to get away. He grabs her by her hair and pulls her closer.

The guys says, "Why do you insist on pissing me off. I'm starting to think you like being punished."

Ashely whimpers in pain and tries to get away. The guys punches her in the gut. She falls, clutching her stomach. The guy steps over her and tries to open the fridge door, but it hits her back as she is on the ground. He closes it a little, then slams it open, hitting her in the back.

The voice comes back. "Are we just going to take this?"

Ashley mutters, "It is my fault."

The voice says, "You deserve better than to be treated like a dog."

Ashely tries to justify in her head, but the pain and his yelling causes her snap. She gets up, and the man pushes her against the wall by her throat. She grabs his arms, and he stares at her eyes. Her hands begin to get hot again. He begins to look uncomfortable as she hangs on to his arms. They begin to burn more and more. He begins to plead with her, almost begging. "Let me go, you dumb bitch."

She ignites all of him to the point he can't even scream because his lungs are collapsing from the heat.

The voice says, excited, "Hold your hand out."

Ashley holds it out, and a sliver spear appears in her hand.

The voice says, "Now finish this filth."

She lets him go, and he falls to his knees, trying to catch his breath. She looks at the rose- colored spear and then lifts it up. He looks up at her as she slams the spear down his throat and through his body. His eyes lose life as his body comes to a standstill, the nerve ending still twitching.

Aten, the doctor, and Violence all sit and watch Ashely's hands catch a blaze. Violence sits down and gets a sinking feeling in stomach. Her hands ignite the table and everything else in the room.

Aten sighs, and the doctor asks, "What is wrong?"

Aten looks at the doctor and replies, "We need to stop using a room for this. This would be the second time that this is completely destroyed, and I'm getting sick of putting it back together."

Violence, already on edge, says, "What did you expect, human? These are forces that you couldn't even imagine. That angel that is coming through right now can ignite the world by herself. Did you not think of the repercussion of what that might do?"

Aten looks at Violence, shocked, and replies, "We did not consider it."

Violence grunts and growls, "Of course. Humanity's actions are like that of newborn children."

The doctor stays, reading the vitals to stay out of it.

Ashley catches her breath, realizing what she has done, and begins to cry.

The voice comes back. "Why are you crying?"

Ashley, sobbing, speaks through the tears. "This has happened before, and I tried to forget it, but this haunts me."

Aphrodite appears before her in her angelic snakelike form.

Ashley looks at her, confused, and stares her up and down.

Aphrodite gives her time.

Ashley gets up and moves toward her, admiring her beautiful rainbow scales. Ashley asks, "May I touch you?"

Aphrodite replies, "Sure."

Ashley touches the scales, feeling the smooth scales, and looks in her eyes. They are rainbow as well. Ashley asks Aphrodite, "What now?"

Aphrodite smiles and says, "I am going to give you choice."

Ashley looks confused.

Aphrodite continues, "You can go to heaven, leaving the body to me, or you can return back to earth and live out your sentence."

Ashley replies quickly, "Not really much of choice."

Aphrodite calmly says, "There is always a choice. What you have done on this earth is not wrong, just unfortunate timing."

Ashley begins to cry again, and Aphrodite holds her close, letting her work through her trauma as she tenderly says, "It's okay, child. The pain can stop, and everything you would ever want and need can be yours. The serenity is intoxicating."

Eventually, she stops crying and says, "I am ready to go to heaven, my angel."

Aphrodite smiles and holds her head against hers as Ashley is turned into a white light, then she is gone. Aphrodite looks at her new body and begins to change it to her liking, making her taller and increasing her muscular system.

When she gets done with her new body, she mutters, "I believe my husband is calling for his death."

She turns her eyes to a magma color and closes her eyes, transporting herself to the world.

10

shley's body wakes up and looks at the charred room. Confused, she stands up, and the sprinkler system goes off, drenching everything in the room.

Aten looks at Violence to do something, and he does. Violence leaves to go confront his wife. Violence walks inside the room, his eyes crimson. He sees Aphrodite for the first in a long time. His eyes begin to turn gold again. She sees him, and her eyes go to a fiery red. He is stuck looking at her as if it is the first time he has ever seen her. She throws a fireball directly at Violence's chest, knocking him back.

Violence, getting knocked back, now has his wits about him again and stands up and yells, "What are you doing?"

Aphrodite responds, "You have a lot more to pay for than that, love!"

Violence summons his shield and slowly walks out.

Aphrodite summons her spear and slams it in the ground, causing a small blaze wave beneath her.

Violence growls, "We have bigger problems here, Aphrodite."

Aphrodite looks at him in a scornful look and says, "It is Wrath now, and what is bigger problem than your ego."

Violence yells, "Atlas."

It catches Wrath off guard as she stops emitting heat and regains her thoughts and responds, "That is impossible."

Violence, looks at the window for any kind of help, but the speaker has been burnt and melted. Violence walks to the glass and breaks it again.

Aten yells, "Can we please stop breaking my building."

Wrath moves closer to Violence, intrigued by the humans.

Wrath snarkily says, "You never liked working with the humans. Why are you now?"

Violence growls back, "Because they need our help."

Wrath looks at Violence, and Violence continues to looks straight to avoid eye contact.

Wrath responds, "Not the whole truth, but we will see soon enough."

Violence says to Aten. "Please, mortal, before I start slaughtering, please show her the footage."

Wrath scoffs and says, "You mean before you start begging for forgiveness and running from the truth again."

Aten grabs a tablet and pulls up the footage and hands it to Wrath.

She watches in disbelief as Atlas tears apart the city. Wrath looks closer and says, "This was Athens."

Violence responds, "It only serves her right."

Aten looks confused, and Wrath clarifies for him, "This is the city that belong to Athena."

The doctor and Aten both look just as confused.

Wrath tries to clarify more, "Just know it is problematic."

Violence looks at her.

Wrath instinctually looks over to Violence and says, "Do not be mad at your sister for winning the competition."

Violence replies, "I brought rivers. She brought an olive. How mad can that be?"

Wrath rolls her eyes.

Aten says, "Can we get out of this place and maybe into a room that is not destroyed?"

Everyone looks around, and everyone is an agreement.

They go to a conference room and take a seat as the doctor puts on the screen a frame of Atlas.

Wrath studies it and looks at Violence, then says, "This should not be possible."

Violence says stoically, "Unfortunately, it is. I do not understand why he is going to Olympus though."

Wrath turns to Aten and says, "Any possibility of you air dropping us there."

Aten responds, "It is possible. However, we just found another unsettling video from a citizen."

He looks over to the doctor, and the doctor puts on the video of Cyclops walking the sand dunes.

Wrath looks stunned as Violence says, "Out of all them, they release the one-eyed headache."

Wrath snaps at him, "Will you please be serious about this."

Violence holds his hands up, not wanting any more attention.

Aten speaks up. "I'm guessing we should be worried."

Wrath responds, "Atlas is a bigger problem. However, Cyclops is a sweetheart but severely follows blindly anyone who cares about him. If we don't get to him before Atlas, he could be weaponized to his cause."

Violence states, "Let's take out Cyclops before dealing with Atlas."

Wrath looks at Violence and states in a deep tone, "We are going to send him back to hell, not execute, if we can help the situation."

Violence looks away, annoyed, as the doctor is writing everything furiously down.

Aten breaks the silence and says, "We should be refueled and ready to go by tomorrow." Aten continues, "Wrath, the doctor will show you to your room. Do I have your guys' word not to rip each other apart."

Violence says in playful voice, "I can keep my hands to myself, but I am not too sure if she can keep her hands off me."

Wrath rolls her eyes and says, "You can only wish, meathead."

Violence gets up and goes to the small gymnasium as Wrath is led to her room.

The doctor comes back to Aten, then says, "I'll put in the work order to fix the room again."

Aten nods and says, "I am not sure how much longer that room is going to hold."

The doctor looks at the camera and sees one of the walls collapse from melting still.

—m—

Violence is in the gym doing push-ups as Wrath walks in and gets on the treadmill. Wrath stares hole into Violence's head, angry, as he does push-ups. Violence feels it, but ignores it as he continues. She starts a walking pace as Violence finishes up. She looks over as he stares at himself in the mirror as he sits down. She begins to smirk at him. He grunts and moves to the bench press as he loads up two plates. She picks up the walking speed to a jog as he begins to push the weight up and up again. He racks it as she jogs, staring at him with anger still.

He finally snaps and asks, "Can I help you?"

She responds coldly, "I do not require your help anymore."

Violence grunts and stares at himself again.

She states, "Staring at yourself will not help."

Violence responds, "This host has a tumor, and I am controlling it."

Wrath responds, "Why did you not eliminate it through the transformation."

Violence responds, "It was not a hindrance."

Wrath quickly says, "Now you are staring at the mirror to no one but yourself."

Violence gets up and unpack the weight and says, "It is okay. I am perfection anyways."

Wrath gets off the treadmill and says, "Far from it, as Adonis was perfection."

Violence begins to push harder, fully enraged. Crimson swirls begin way off the bar as she smirks as she leaves. Violence looks around annoyed and realizes she has done nothing but play her mind games and goes back to his workout.

The next day they wake up, and Violence is waiting for the helicopter with Aten and the doctor. She shows up with a coffee in hand. Violence smells the air and recognizes almond, hazelnut, and sugar.

He says, "You are late. We have been waiting for you."

She looks at him in disgust and responds, "The time was not disclosed, so how could I be there on time?"

Violence snaps back, "By reading the room."

The helicopter starts the spin as Violence walks toward it. Wrath looks at him in disgust, not realizing he is playing her own mind games against her. She get annoyed and walks to the helicopter. They hop on the helicopter, and Aten says over the comms, "This will take you to the Cyclops. God speed."

Violence answers, "I never needed his speed, but I appreciate the notion."

The helicopter begins to take off, and the doctor says to Aten, "Do you think all angels have drama going on?"

Violence hops on the comms and responds, "Yes."

Aten looks at the doctor and turns off his microphone. Aten responds to the doctor, "Apparently."

The doctor takes his mic off and looks at Aten and asks, "When are we going to tell him about the other mask?"

Aten looks at him confused. "What other mask?"

The doctor, trying to read Aten, says, "You're right. What other one?" as the doctor smiles.

Aten responds, "Seriously, what other mask?"

The doctor looks confused. "The one that we just acquired before Wrath. You know, the one that was flew in months after Violence?"

Aten says, "Fuck, I forgot about that one."

The doctor looks like he has just seen a ghost and says, "Well, we are dead as soon as he finds out."

The helicopter ride was uncomfortably quiet as Violence and Wrath have so much to say, but no one wants to begin to open up the subject that is brewing.

The reach another military base and is met with a major.

The major opens up the door and says, "Aten has directed me to lead you to a plane that will get you to where you need to go."

Violence stares at the major, his eyes piercing his soul, and it makes the major visibly uncomfortable. The major leads him to the plane, and Violence and Wrath file into the plane. You can hear him sigh in relief as the plane shuts and they take off to their destination.

Wrath stares at Violence as Violence closes his eyes. Eventually, she breaks the silence.

"We just going to be silent the whole trip?"

Violence responds, "I was hoping."

Wrath answers back under her breath, "I was hoping as well."

Violence ignores it as she fidgets, trying to get comfortable.

She breaks the silence again and asks, "Can I ask you one question?"

Violence grunts in defeat.

Wrath rolls her eyes and says, "That's not a word."

Violence open his eyes up at her and stares into her fiery red eyes and says, "I would rather you did not, but if it will help you in calming your mind, then do so."

Wrath sighs and responds, "Never mind."

Violence lets it sit for a while, then curiosity get the better of him as he asks, "What is the question?"

Wrath responds, "No, you are right."

Violence responds, "It will not leave my head."

Wrath smiles at him and says, "Ask me nicely."

Violence summons a kopis, and Wrath's flames begin to dance around her fingers in anticipation.

Violence finally mutters, "Pray and tell me what is on your mind."

Wrath smiles. "You could never tell me no. However, did you ever think of me?"

Violence quickly lies, "Never."

Wrath sees that he is lying and smiles.

The pilot yells, "Thirty seconds to drop!"

Violence responds in a low tone, "Fucking finally." He gets up and straps his parachute once Wrath does the same. He waits and says, "I miss my wings."

The green light goes off, and they jump out over the sands of the desert.

They hit the sand dunes, and Aten open the communication as they watch ahead with a drone.

"Three miles north. He is digging into the sand."

Violence looks at Wrath, confused. She notices the look and points to a direction. He looks at the direction and begins walking in the general direction. As they get closer, they begin to feel the ground beneath them quake. They stop and look around. Violence looks at Wrath, then signals for her to get closer. She does, so unsure of what is going on. Violence puts his hand to the ground and pulses the ground and sees a group of giant scorpions taking position for an ambush. Wrath sees it as well as she puts her hand on his shoulder, seeing everything he sees. She looks down at Violence and sees a silver chain. She stares at the chain to see what it is.

Violence stands up, breaking her concentration, and he asks, "What would you say is the proper way to go about this?"

Wrath thinks and says, "Throw your weapon in the middle. That might cause them to attack at nothing."

Violence summons a spear, and he throws it in the middle of them, hitting the sand. They all pop out of the sand and swarm the spear. Wrath sees them and lets a blaze loose on them, searing the majority of them as two escape underground. Violence sees a trail going toward him as he summons his kopis. He waits for it to get closer, then he leaps toward it and digs his kopis deep in the ground, catching the scorpion as it tries to get away. He lifts it out of the ground as Wrath bury her spear in the underbelly of the scorpion, killing it. Violence drops the scorpion and sees a trail dangerously close to Wrath. He pushes her out of the way as it jumps up. It lands on Violence and tries to sting him multiple times. He uses his braces and cuts the tail point off. It screeches in pain as Wrath buries the spear on the head of the scorpion. The scorpion dies, and she pulls the spear back as she hears Violence grunt in pain.

She stops and asks, "What are you crying about now?"

Violence says in pain, "Your spear head is in my chest. Looks like revenge is yours."

Wrath looks and sees a little magma blood on the sand. She begins to panic. Wrath quickly says, "I am sorry."

Violence begins to laugh as she pulls the scorpion off him with her spear. She looks at him pissed but relieved.

He smiles and says, as his eyes are glowing gold, "Never gets old."

She gets angry and hits him with a fire bolt to the chest. As it hits him, he flies back and slowly gets back gets up. Violence says, catching his breath, "Okay, that one was real."

She starts glaring at him for making a horrible joke as they begin to feel the ground quake. He looks up and sees Cyclops has come to investigate what the sounds were.

Cyclops see Ares and Aphrodite and gets a disconcerting look on his face, like he is found guilty of doing something wrong.

Violence steps up, and Wrath stops him and whispers, "Let me handle this."

Violence shrugs and whispers back, "I did not wish to talk to him anyways. It hurts my head."

Wrath rolls her eyes as she turns around to talk to Cyclops.

Wrath says, "What are you doing out here, Cyclops?"

Cyclops remains quiet as he look around, like he cannot hear her.

She repeats, "Cyclops, look at me."

Cyclops looks at her as she continues, "What are you doing out here?"

Cyclops responds, "Playing in the sun and sand."

Wrath responds, "Who let you out?"

Cyclops looks around again, not sure what to say, then tries to lie. "The Father let me out."

Wrath looks at him with disappointment and responds, "We both know that is a lie, my friend."

Cyclops looks down in shame and says, "My friend Atlas."

Wrath responds, "You know you are not supposed to be out here. It is dangerous."

Cyclops responds quickly, "I will be careful."

Wrath smiles and says, "I know, but it's not you who we are trying to protect. It's the other people who will try to hurt you."

Cyclops looks confused. "Cyclops does not want to hurt them. Why would they hurt me?"

Violence begins to get agitated and takes a deep breath.

Wrath says, "Listen, we need to get you back to where you come from."

Cyclops tears up a little and responds, "I do not want to go back. They are mean to me down there."

Wrath can sense the hurt in his voice as she says, "What if you go to my circle where no will be mean to you until I can figure out something?"

Cyclops retorts, "They are mean. They call me one eye one brain cell."

Violence chuckles a bit, and Cyclops sees it and begins to get mad.

Violence try to smooth it over by saying, "You have to admit, Cyclops, it is pretty funny."

Cyclops get angry and yells, then swings his club and hit Wrath, knocking her back.

Violence watches as she flies back and stares at Cyclops with death in his eyes.

—◊◊◊—

Back at base, Commander Hawke is in the vents looking for answer and mapping her route as she goes. She moves quietly as she eavesdrops in the conversation about the other mask. She hears the voice, "Go right." She looks around scared at what she just heard. She looks to her right and begins to quietly move that way. She passes guards till she begins to feel an energy around her. Hawke looks around, feeling like she is not alone. She sees a door that is guarded by two.

"That's where our answers are."

She slowly moves above them and looks around, then drops on one, knocking him out with her drop. The other guard reacts quickly and kicks Hawke in the wall. The guard pulls his weapon up and pulls the trigger, but the weapon is jammed. Hawke pulls out cables from her back pocket and moves to subdue the guard. The guards tries to hit her with rifle stock. She dodges it and moves behind him and gets the cable around his neck and pulls till he is subdued. She opens the door and takes the guards with her. She steps in a dark red room. She walks to the center and sees a mask sparkling the glass it is being held in. She hears the voice again.

"Put it on. There is not time to waste."

Hawke looks around, unsure about it.

The voice comes back. "I am Athena, an angel. I have led you to this moment. Trust me and I will not betray you. You will have everything you want and more."

Hawke mind begins to race of everything she ever wanted in the world.

"To be a mother, have a good husband."

She begins to tear up as she sees what would make her happy.

The voice comes back. "Now is not the time for tears. Save those tears for tears of joy."

Hawke snaps out it and opens the glass. As she holds the mask, she begins to feel at home, true comfort. She puts it on, and lightning comes out of her, tearing the room apart as the room goes dark. The only thing that shows in the room is Athena's eyes as the glow a white-blue lightning.

Aten and the doctor come around the corner to see what the alarm is going off for, and they see a tall, slender woman step out, sparks of lightning coming off her hands.

Aten sighs and says, "Which one are you?"

Athena looks at Aten and replies, "I am God's balance, my father's glory, and apparently my brother's keeper."

The doctor looks at Aten and says, "So this is Violence's babysitter?"

Athena rolls her eyes and states, "I am Athena, and I believe you have met part of the family already."

The doctor looks at Aten as he says, "Violence is going to kill us."

Athena steps closer as she says, "He will not. He will finally hear reason, or feel my bolt."

Aten looks at the doctor and can see the doctor is in love.

The doctor says, "Okay, I believe whatever you say."

11

Violence screams, "Wrath," while looking at her general direction. Cyclops looks at what he has done and begins to stammer. "I-I-I..."

Violence hears his voice get cranky and sends himself into a rage. Violence turns around quickly and jumps up Cyclops's leg to his face and punches Cyclops in the nose. The crimson blast makes Cyclops stagger and take a knee to keep from falling.

Cyclops yells, "That hurt."

Violence cannot hear anything he is saying as he runs to Cyclops.

Cyclops regains his thoughts and tosses a wave of sand, blocking Violence's view as Cyclops moves. Violence runs through the sand as he tries to cover his eyes. Cyclops slams his club at Violence and barely misses but shakes the ground beneath Violence. Violence gets low in a defensive position as he targets Cyclops. Violence summons his spear as he sees the giant. Cyclops runs to Violence, lifting his club. Violence hurls the spear at Cyclops's bicep. It pierces deep in Cyclops's bicep, making him stop and tend to the spear. Cyclops grabs the spear. It starts to tear away at his hand, trying to pull it away. Violence open his hand, making the spear blade become jagged.

Cyclops cries out loud in pain. "Atlas, my friend, where are you?"

Violence, lost in the moment, replies, "No one will save you from me."

Cyclops continues to cry out, "My friend, please."

Violence summons his chain, then throws it at Cyclops's feet and begins to run around, making his feet trapped in the chain. Cyclops is too focused on the blade in his arm he doesn't feel the chain. Violence makes a couple of loops and pulls with all of his strength, making Cyclops fall and hit a rock, unconscious. Violence waits to see if it is a trap and cautiously walks on top of Cyclops and begins to feel the rage again. He begins pounding Cyclops's chest with his fist as he tries to reach his heart. He finally hears a crack, but he is hit with a firebolt, pushing him off.

Violence lies on the sand, out of breath, as Wrath goes to examine Cyclops. She looks him over, and he is barely breathing. She puts his head on chest and can hear his lungs filling with blood. She looks at Violence as he barely starts to get up. She begins to walk to him aggressive, as she feels anger. Violence tries to get up, his ear ringing, and can see Wrath walking toward him. He tries to stand up, and he stumbles from the firebolt. She reaches him as he tries to get up. She looks him over and can see the firebolt burned him pretty well. She puts his head up and looks at his gold eyes. Her eyes turn a rainbow color as a white light starts to flow to his chest. His wounds begin to heal as she smiles. He becomes coherent again and notices what is happening.

He grunts, "It isn't what you think."

Wrath smiles and replies, "Sure it isn't."

Violence gets up completely and sees she has her ring on her hand still. They hear a piercing and a last breath. They look over and see a tall spike of ice going through Cyclops's chest. Limbo walks around the dead giant as he approaches Violence and Wrath. Limbo takes a looks at Wrath and tries to speak.

"My lady…hello."

Violence stares at Limbo and says, "Stop drooling. You are making me depressed."

Limbo snaps out of it and tries to cover it up by saying, "The Cyclops took a lot of energy, Violence, not all of us can go on pure rage."

Wrath can feel Violence's temper about to go off again as she says, "We can talk about this back at base."

Limbo looks at Wrath suspiciously as he asks, "What do you mean base?"

Violence grunts as he says, "We are working with the humans on this one."

Limbo looks at Violence, puzzled, as he asks, "I thought you hate the humans."

Violence continues to stare at Limbo. "Why does everyone think I hate the humans?"

Wrath gets tired of the conversation and states, "We will talk about this back at base." Wrath pushes her mic and calls for an extraction.

Limbo says, "By the way, the Cyclops killed a watcher, and I managed to retrieve his horn though." Limbo reaches behind him and takes out a horn made of ivory.

Wrath looks at Violence, concerned, as Violence looks at the horn.

Violence continues, "Looks like someone tried to send the Cyclops back before we did."

The helicopter shows up, and Violence and Wrath start getting in as Limbo stops. Violence takes a seat, and Wrath is also about to sit when she sees Limbo standing there.

Wrath says, "What are you waiting for?"

Limbo responds, "What is this vehicle?"

Violence grunts as Wrath answers, "It a vehicle. Get in so we can take you back to our area of operation."

Limbo begins to get in cautiously and takes a seat next to Violence. Violence looks at him in annoyance. Limbo looks at him, then at the ground. The helicopter takes off, and the ride is as silent as the grave.

Limbo breaks the silence by commenting, "You could cut the tension with a knife right now."

Violence summons a kopis and looks at Limbo. Wrath's flame begins to dance around her finger. Limbo reads the room, then goes back to being silent.

They land back at base as soldier come to tell them that they are to report to the conference room immediately.

Violence replies, "Say it to me in that tone again and I'll send you to report in hell."

The soldier stands back and walks away.

Wrath says, "Would it kill you to make some friends?"

Violence responds, "I thought we were friends. We just had a nice conversation all the way here." He begins to walk in the base as the rest follows. He starts to slow down as he can feel another presence in the same area. Wrath and Limbo notice his instincts are going.

Wrath asks, "What is it?"

Violence responds, "I do not know, but there is another in soul in there, and it feels well responsible." Violence summons his blade and walks in and begins to move his chair. The chair spins as he gets closer.

Athena turns all the way around and says, "Good to see you again, brother. I can see you are still making a mess everywhere you go."

Violence put his weapon away and retorts, "It's under control."

Athena sees the rest of them and says, "Hello."

Wrath walks in nervously. She can feel Athena's eyes following her everywhere she goes. Wrath turns to her and says, "What do you want?"

Athena responds, "I want to know why you are all here."

Violence responds, "It is not of your concern, dearest sister."

Athena responds aggressively, "It is my concern when my brother manages to get back on earth, even though he made a mess about angels interfering with earth."

Violence smiles and takes a seat and responds, "It was not a mess, it was a statement."

Athena snarls and responds, "You took heaven to war."

Violence hold up a finger and responds, "I did not just take heaven to war. I won, and there I made a statement."

Athena starts to speak louder. "And yet here you are, brother."

The word "brother" sounded with thunder as Violence looks at her, unfazed.

Wrath speaks up. "We are here because the Titans are loose and on the earth."

Athena looks at here, concerned, then says to Violence, "Brother, please tell me this harlot is lying."

Wrath looks at her, hurt by her words.

Violence reacts in aggressive tone. "Show some respect, dearest sister. It is partially your fault for being such an inconsistent coward."

Athena turns to Violence, stunned by his words.

Violence continues, "If you could get your hands dirty more than once or better yet interfering and stopping the angels from doing what is necessary to secure the world, then you are nothing but a coward that hides behind the name of justice."

Athena looks down and thinks back to when Ares was going to kill the Titans in their cell. She changes from aggressive to ashamed for being wrong.

Athena says somberly, "I apologize to both of you for being aggressive. You have spoken truth, brother." Athena looks over to Wrath. "I apologize for my words. Your husband truly does care."

Wrath looks at Violence, confused on why he would defend her.

Violence proceeds to say, slowly calming down, "It's not about that anymore. If we are going to stop them, then we must work as a team and show respect regardless of how messed up a family we are. This is more than about us now."

Athena looks at Wrath and says, "Apologies, my anger got the better of me."

Wrath nods, trying to keep the peace.

Limbo speaks up. "I am glad to be part of this family."

Violence sighs and responds, "I lost my new hope...thank you for that."

—m—

Atlas walks into Mount Olympus and looks around. He walks around muttering to himself. He begins to feel a shadow presence behind him. He continues as if he does not feel it. Atlas looks over cliff as he feels the presence getting closer. A shadowlike form comes closer as Atlas gets annoyed and says, "Can we skip the theatrics and get into it?"

A shadow takes a dark female human form and stands next to Atlas. The shadow asks, "How did you know?"

Atlas calmly replies, "I am a Titan, not your peers. Do not underestimate me, slave."

The form stands there like a statue and thinks.

Atlas continues, "What is your name, slave?"

The form says, "I am no slave, but I am sure you are talking to me, and I will not be rude. My name is Ares."

Atlas pauses a moment and sighs, "I do not know who you are."

Ares stares at him as Atlas looks back. Ares gets a shock after staring at Atlas.

Atlas turns away and walks away while saying, "You are not going to survive this."

Ares falls back into the floor as Atlas keeps walking. Atlas is hit with a sharp pain in his heart as he hears Cyclops crying for his help. Atlas tries to open his hand to set a portal to him, but he feels the Cyclops fall and is silent.

Atlas thinks, *I am sorry, my friend.* Atlas looks and screams, "You are no God, Zeus! You are a child, and as long as I walk the earth, you are forever in jeopardy from being the sham God. I will devour you like our father!" Atlas takes a deep breath as the thunder sounds from his yell. He thinks and regains his control and takes a deep breath and remembers his plans. He takes a seat on a rock to grieve for his friend Cyclops.

12

The next morning comes, and Violence is doing an arms workout as Athena walks in and says, "Why do you work out? Nothing gets bigger, my insecure older brother. We are angels."

Violence has his earbuds in, listening to his music. As he sees Athena talking, he takes an earbud out and nods his heads up in a question.

She shakes her head and keeps walking to the cafeteria.

He puts his earbud back in as he sees Wrath walking around with a coffee. He takes deep breath and smells all the aromas again as he looks at the clock and begins to keep a mental note of when everyone wakes up. He sees Limbo walk out as he tries to wave to Violence in a friendly motion. Violence looks at him disgusted and flips him off, then turns his back and begins working on the other side. Limbo looks surprised, but he know he should not be as he walks into the cafeteria. Limbo turns the corner and sees Wrath and Athena eating at different tables even though there are only two of them. He gets his food and then is stuck with a weird choice of which table to eat. He feels eyes staring him down as he wants to sit with Wrath and her beauty but is afraid of Athena and her power.

He thinks, *I am going to go eat with the animal in the gym.*

They watch him leave as the blame each other in their mind. Limbo returns to the gym and sees Violence taking a rest between sets. He finds a bench to eat his microwaved waffle. Violence sees Limbo and laughs a little. Limbo, not familiar with Violence showing joy, begins to get comfortable and cautiously asks, "What are you laughing about?"

Violence takes an earbud out and says, "Is it really that bad in there?"

Limbo responds in a smile. "I would rather walk on broken glass than be in there."

Violence quickly says, "Give it time. The volcano will erupt soon enough."

Limbo enjoys his meal in peace, feeling oddly safe in Violence's presence.

Limbo finished his meal and looks at Violence curling weights. He gets up and says, ashamed, "Thank you for this peace."

Violence continues his workout, ignoring him as he turns to leave. Violence sets his weights down and says in a low voice, "Be careful who you trust, brother. Sometimes they will try to stab you in the back."

Limbo feels like Violence is looking at his soul as he leaves.

The doctor finds the group and says, "Aten would like you guys in the conference room. We may have found something that is of interest."

They get up and go to the conference room. As they take their seats, Aten turns on a screen, and it shows a map of Mexico. Violence looks at it closer and sees it is the pyramid. He smiles as he sits back. Wrath sees Violence's smile as she looks down, then looks at Athena, who looks annoyed.

Aten can sense the weird tension and stays silent for a minute, then he finally breaks the silence. "What is it? Someone speak up now."

Violence smuggles looks to Athena and says, "Would you like to?" He looks at Wrath, then says, "Or would you?"

Athena finally breaks and says, "It is the Aztecs blood sacrifice, my brother's third race of people driven by blood."

Violence sits back and says, "The biggest empire landwise was founded by ego."

Athena says sharply back "They did not last long against the Spanish, did they?"

Violence sits up and replies, "You're forgetting, some of those Spanish were from my Spartans lineage."

Wrath tries to intervene. "Bickering will not tell us why we are looking at the pyramid of Mexico."

Violence says sarcastically, "If I had to guess, it is because Atlas has a taste for craftsmanship, and that's where the next mask is."

Aten looks at Violence and says, "How did you know?"

Violence looks at Aten and replies, "What my partners failed to see is that we give off a different energy, almost a different vibration."

The doctor begins typing on his laptop and gets Aten's attention.

Athena and Wrath look at Violence, curious on how he figured this out, as Violence continues, "It looks like deadly radiation. However, it's just the frequency we all work on. I cannot track, but I know of it, and it looks like our friend Atlas can see the vibration somehow."

They have already launched a drone, and they see Atlas tearing a Mexican cartel and military apart, and the other military begins to retreat. Violence sees him tearing the tank apart, beginning to look for weaknesses.

Athena can feel Violence working on something as she says, "Please be patient, my brother. We do not need another bronze-jar moment."

Violence snaps his head and stares at her, then says in growl, "Funny, I do not recall anyone else doing anything to stop them."

Wrath has to interrupt again as she says, "When do we take off?"

Aten cautiously says, "The transport is being fueled and ready to go in ten. Gear up and get ready. If you see Atlas, you have kill on sight. Good hunting, squad."

Violence growls and gets up and walks away as the rest follow suit, preparing for what might come.

Violence is the first to stand in the hangar, then Athena follows shortly after. She stands by his side and sighs.

He cautiously asks, "What is wrong now?"

Athena responds, "Please do not do anything rash, my brother."

Violence looks at her, then smiles and says, "No promises, my lovely sister."

The other angels walk in, and Wrath stands next to Violence as she asks, "Please, will you be cautious for our sake."

Athena looks at Wrath, then says, "That's what I just asked him."

Violence begins to look annoyed and snaps back, "I will, but if you show any hesitation, I will act."

Wrath looks at him, worried, as Athena looks at Limbo. Limbo looks scared as he has never met a Titan.

Athena, trying to calm his nerves, says, "The are fallen gods, younger brother. Do not be afraid."

Limbo tries to pretend he is not disturbed by a Titan as he says, "I am not concerned about a Titan."

Athena sees the lie in his eyes as she lets the subject go.

The plane lands, and they head to get on it.

Upon arriving, they get off the plane and runs through the city's streets as they see military trying to escort them out of the city as it lies in ruin.

Athena looks around as she says commandingly, "We would cover more ground if we split up."

Violence, taking what the group has asked him in the helicopter, stays silent and listens.

Athena says, "Me and Wrath take the left. You and Limbo take right. Clean up any resistance on the way."

Wrath and Athena look at each other, seeing if they can trust each other as Violence speaks up.

"Me and Wrath. You two will kill each other."

Limbo responds quickly, "Me and Wrath should be partners as we don't have to worry about each other."

He gets ignored as Violence and Athena are having a stare down about who is calling the shots.

Athena finally breaks the stare and says, "I'll let you have this one, brother. Limbo, with me now."

Wrath looks at Violence, curious, as they start moving through the city. They see a young woman looking into a pit covered by a truck that is flipped over. Wrath rushes over as Violence watches her try to lift the truck to no avail. Violence walks next to the truck and watches.

Wrath finally snaps, "Are you going to help?"

Violence smirks and says cockily, "Only if you ask nicely."

Wrath whispers, "You useless brute. She does not have much more time left before she is poisoned."

Violence looks at her and motions her to move out of the way as Violence lifts the truck up, allowing the girl to get out and to safety with her partner.

Wrath looks at Violence in disgust as Violence goes to women and says, "Donde esta demonio?"

Wrath looks at him and asks, "Why are you saying it in Spanish?"

Violence looks at Wrath and responds, "Would you rather me say it in Latin?"

Wrath looks at him stupidly as she says, "They speak English."

Violence looks at the women as one speaks up. "I do."

Wrath looks at him and says, "Not everyone here only speaks Spanish."

Violence looks back at the women. "Where is the big monster?"

Wrath cannot help herself as she says, "Que?"

Violence looks back her as the girls start laughing at them. Violence looks back at the women as one of them says, "You guys have been married for a while?"

Violence grunts as he follows the path of most destruction as Wrath goes up to the women and says, "Mucho tiempo, señoritas. Mochas gracias."

They giggle as she follows Violence down his path.

They meet up at a singular point as they approach the temples. They begin to see several other tracks.

Athena studies them and is dumbfounded. She gets up and says questioningly, "I have no knowledge of these tracks. These are not of this plane, almost like they were made."

Violence looks at them and studies them as he says, "They are demons made by Lucifer himself. Is that who let Atlas out?"

Limbo looks around as he slinks to the back, trying to remain unseen.

Athena responds quickly, "Our father removed that possibility when you entered hell."

Violence looks at Athena and says, "It's not like we could leave our realm anyways."

Athena looks around and sees Limbo but staying silent. She thinks there is no harm in Limbo as he had that power revoked as well.

Violence starts moving forward to see what is to come.

Athena stops him and questions him, "What are you doing?"

Violence looks at her in confusion as he says, "Moving forward. As much as I love standing in the woods with all of you, I rather be somewhere else."

Athena responds, "Can we talk about this for a minute?"

Violence argues back, "What more should we talk about?"

Athena looks at Wrath for help, as Wrath agrees. "We should know more about this before we move."

Violence sees his is outnumbered. He thinks back to the trip here, and he gave his word not to be rash with his choices. He stands down and looks at Athena and says, "What do you suggest?"

Athena looks around and can't think of anything as she looks to Wrath and sees she is just as clueless.

Violence looks at both of them and says, "I am going to assume we have no idea?"

Athena looks down in acceptance.

Violence moves forward and sees a soldier from hell. He turns back to them and says, "I think I have found out what those tracks were."

Athena goes where Violence is and sees the hell soldier. She looks at Violence and whispers, "How did they get out?"

Violence looks at her in sarcasm. "Maybe they are sightseeing."

Wrath butts in and whispers, "Now is not the time for sarcasm."

Violence responds to her and says, "Nor is it the time for stupid question, but here we are."

Athena looks at him in disgust.

Limbo takes a look and sees the soldier and looks for anything that can help him. Athena and Violence notice Limbo looking for something, and they both take a mental note of it. Violence puts his hands on the ground as he pulses the ground, seeing several heartbeats and one slow heartbeat. Wrath touches his shoulder too see what he is seeing and notices the slowing heartbeat.

Violence lets go of the ground as he says, "Five soldiers and something else. They caught someone or something."

Athena looks worried.

Violence notices this and asks, "What is it?"

Athena thinks for a minute and finally says, "This was another watchers' station. Is Atlas targeting the watchers?"

Violence thinks for a moment. "It would make sense. By definition, the only other Titan in play right now is our father."

Athena thinks and responds, "He is taking out this plane's protection."

Violence nods as he stands up and summons his kopis and shield.

Wrath looks at him and says, "No rash decisions."

Violence responds, annoyed, "I am just preparing for the inevitable."

Athena looks annoyed and then sighs as she summons her spear. The group gets there weapons ready. Violence summons his black-and-gold helmet as he looks at the rest. He turns the corner and is faced with a demon. As they stare each other, Violence slices into the demon, and it lets off a deafening shriek, alarming the rest. Athena thrust her spear in the face of the demon.

Athena looks at Violence in irritation as Violence moves in and runs to the closest demon. Wrath follows closely out of instinct. Athena lets loose a thunderbolt, turning one of them into ash, as she pursues another one. Limbo lets loose an ice wall, knocking one down, as Wrath and Violence make quick work of two. Violence slides underneath the first one as the demon turns to follow Violence. As he slides, Wrath thrusts her sword onto the demon's head, slicing it off as it falls down. Violence continues to slide, catching the next demon off guard as he slices the demon's leg, cutting it off, as Wrath lets loose a fireball through the chest, and it grunts. Violence turns around with the kopis cleaving the demon in half. They look to the other to see where they are at. Violence can't help but look at Wrath in bewilderment as she stands, a walking embodiment of love. She catches his gaze, and she stares back, and then they hear Limbo grunt. That breaks their stare as Violence moves to help Limbo take care of his demon.

They make their way to a pyramid. They begin to feel the ground tremble beneath them as Atlas comes out of the temple with Gluttony and a watcher angel who is barely clinging on to life as he bleeds out a silver liquid. Gluttony sees his old comrades as he holds the horn of the watcher. The group look in horror as they see Gluttony hold it with pride if he just accomplished something.

Violence speaks out. "You are a disgrace to our father."

Gluttony responds, "We will be gods once again. All the something our father would never let us be again. Then Ares I am coming for you. The disgrace to us all." She begins to tear up as she says thru tears "Then I will come for your daughter, and you will know my agony, my grief, my torture."

Athena responds in anger, "Because of our choices, we were made as gods, and you are proving our father's point."

Gluttony goes to speak up and argue, but Atlas comes out and says in a deep voice, "Do not continue to argue with sheep that were meant to be slaughtered. Why should a peasant know the language of a king?"

Violence looks at Atlas with fire in his eyes ready for combat as Atlas looks at Violence with anticipation.

13

Atlas looks over everybody and deems them not a threat as he pulls out one of the four horns.

He says quietly, "After all this time, with all I have lost, it pains me to see the vermin your father calls his children muck up the very place that was supposed to be my home."

Athena responds, "It was never yours to begin with, Atlas. You are too report back to Taurus, and we shall be merciful. I give you my word."

Atlas looks at Athena and says, "I am guessing you are the younger one, the just one."

Violence smiles and snickers as Atlas turns to Violence and says, "I am guessing you are the older one, the one full of mistakes that the younger one seeks to redeem."

Violence stares as his smile leaves as Wrath moves to Violence.

Atlas sees this and stares at her. "You are not an angel. You are a Titan, a very beautiful at that as well. I shall make you my wife when I am done with conquering."

Violence summons his chain out of anger and throws it at Atlas's neck, but Atlas catches it in a swift motion. He yanks the chain, and Violence comes flying to Atlas. Atlas catches him by his breastplate and looks him in the eyes as he whispers, "Chains work both ways." Atlas throws Violence into the temple as Violence breaks the walls, leaning into the temple with his back.

Athena sees this and moves to a guarded position.

Atlas summons a portal as he says, "Come, my friends, we have work to do still."

Athena yells, "We will never join."

Gluttony walks through the portal as Wrath and Athena see Limbo move to the portal.

Athena says, confused, "What are you doing?"

Limbo looks back at her and says unsure, "Joining the side that wants me." The angel crawls to safety as to be hidden.

Violence beaks through the temple again, coming outside to regain his position as he sees Limbo and Gluttony walk to Atlas as a friend. Violence runs over to Wrath as Athena loses her temper and charges Atlas with her sword. She gets close enough to swing her sword, but Atlas punches her in the chest, making her fly back. Atlas summons his sword and begins moving toward them as a trident comes flying out of the woods and hits Atlas in the back. He turns around wincing in pain. He pulls it out and throws it back at the direction, then looks at Limbo and commands him, "Summon an ice dome around Ares and Aphrodite."

Limbo looks at her and obeys his new master.

Athena gets up as Atlas holds his hands together, and white light comes between them. As he finishes putting them together, they hear a thud in the dome. Athena stops and looks at the murky ice. She can see something large in there. She gains her focus as she looks at Atlas as she portals away with Limbo and Gluttony. Heresy comes out of the wood and stands, catching his breath. Athena stares at him as he looks like a water lumberjack. He catches his breath as Athena comes up to him and greets him.

"Poseidon, how are you, my nephew?"

Poseidon looks around and says, "It's Heresy now. I fell into the depths of hells as well, but that is a story for another time."

In the ice dome, Wrath is behind Violence as they look and see a sleeping Hydra. Wrath squeezes Violence shoulder in fear as Violence moves her more to the left.

She whispers, "Is that a—"

Violence cuts her off and whispers back, "My mother and sister's creation."

Wrath looks at it sleeping soundly. As she begins to examine their situation, she whispers, "I thought Hercules killed it."

Violence looks at her in irritation as to say, "Clearly not."

Wrath continues to look as Violence remains fixed on the Hydra. Wrath squeezes Violence shoulder to get his attention and whispers, "I am going to have to burn a way out for us."

Violence looks at her in shock as it is a risky plan not to wake the Hydra.

Wrath looks at him in desperation as they are out of options.

Violence nods to do it.

She whispers, "I'll try to be quite." She holds her hand to make a small flame and puts it on the wall of the dome and tries and melt the ice.

Athena and Poseidon try to look in the ice and can't see anything of use. She looks at Poseidon with a grim look.

He looks back at her, thinking the same thing, as he says, "We shouldn't."

Athena says calmly, "I do not see any other way."

Poseidon looks over the ice again as he sighs and says, "I do not believe this to be the right course of action, but if you insist, I shall aid."

Athena eyes begin to swirl electrically as she focuses on the ice, then she lets go a huge lightning bolt on the tip of the ice dome. As it strikes, she hears a familiar roar from inside. Her eyes start to widen to the knowledge. She begins to hurl more lightning bolts as hard and as swift as she can. Poseidon can see her stress over the roar and begins to try and dig with his trident, not really doing much as the dying angel crawls toward Athena, leaving a little silver blood trail.

Wrath is making little progress with the flame as Violence stands guard, watching the sleeping Hydra. He hears a giant boom on top of the dome, and he can see a bright light hit it and awakens the Hydra. Wrath stops and looks at the Hydra as it stretches its long neck, scales, and back into place. It hums to life as it looks at Wrath and Violence. It roars a shrieking sound as it lays claim to its new territory. Violence summon a spear and puts his kopis in the ground, readying himself for combat, as another bright light hits the top of the dome again, making it more frenzied than before.

Violence looks back and points his spear at top of the dome and yells, "Burn the roof!"

Wrath wastes no time as she lets a steady flow of flame at the top of the roof as the Hydra gets ready to attack. Violence stares down the Hydra as it snaps at Violence close to where they are trying to identify the opponent. Violence doesn't take the bait. The Hydra starts to emit a green cloud from its body as it snaps closer to Violence.

Violence jabs back, poking it with the spear tip. The Hydra recoils back, surprised by the cut as it snaps fully at Violence but is met and pierced by Violence's spear. The spear gets stuck in the Hydra's mouth as it pulls back. The Hydra fumbles its mouth as it tries to get free from the spear as a mother bright light hits the dome. The Hydra slams its mouth shut, snapping the spear.

Violence picks up his kopis and gets ready for round two. The Hydra snaps again like a viper as Violence swings his kopis up, slicing the Hydra's bottom lip. As it gets more aggressive, it screeches again. It tries to stomp Violence as he dodges by rolling away. Violence sees an opening, and he slices the leg, cutting it. As it falls away, he runs to it and begins to cleave the neck. As the neck breaks free, he hears Wrath scream, "What are you doing!"

Violence looks confused as he says cautiously, "Killing it?"

Wrath stares as the Hydra grows two more heads.

Violence turns around to see as he yells, "Stay down!"

The Hydra stands again, now with two heads. One of the heads snaps at Violence as he cleaves it again, and the Hydra staggers.

Wrath screams, "Stop cutting the head off!"

Violence looks confused as he asks, "How do I kill it then?"

One of the heads swoops, knocking Violence into an ice wall as Wrath continues to burn the roof. Violence hits the ice hard as the Hydra tries to strike again. Violence punches it down, knocking the head to the ground. He slams his kopis, piercing the Hydra's head to the ground, yelling at it, "Stay there!"

Violence makes his way back to Wrath as he picks up his shield.

The other two heads spawn and look at the Hydra's head stapled to the ground.

Violence summons a gladius. The Hydra looks at the incapacitated head and looks back at Violence, and both strike at the same time. Violence curls behind his shield as a mouth grips the shield. The other one flies over the other head as the other head pulls the shield away. Violence summons a chain as the shield is pulled away. Violence swings the chain, prepared to snap, as the heads strike again. Violence swings the chain, hitting one, as the other head goes above again, striking Wrath. She screams in pain as Violence turns, slicing the Hydra's throat as it recoils in pain. Violence hurries to Wrath and looks at the black wound on her thigh. As it throbs, Wrath winces in pain. The lighting hits again, causing a crack in the dome. Violence hears the beast come back to finish the job as his eyes glow a dark-red crimson. He turns and faces the beast. The Hydra looms over them. As the Hydra strikes again, Violence pommels strikes as the crimson burst leaves the pommel. He dodges the other head as he throws the gladius, catching on the heads, pinning it to the wall. As the last head looms over at an unarmed Violence, it strikes. He catches the jaws, holding it open. Violence feels a warm presence washing him as he turns around and sees Wrath giving the rest of power to him. He looks at her in despair as he steps on her hand, breaking it.

Wrath exclaims, "What? Why!"

Violence replies, "No!" He stomps on the Hydra's bottom fang, ripping it out as it tries to recoil in pain. Violence does not release his grip as a lightning bolt finally breaks through, searing the head off as the other heads rip through Violence's blades. The other heads screech in pain as the ice cracks all the way down, giving Violence and Wrath an exit. Violence picks up Wrath and makes his escape. As he leaves, he sees Athena, Poseidon, and the dying angel. He rushes her over the dying angel as he regroups with the others.

Athena and Poseidon continue to try and break free Violence and Wrath as a dying angel crawls to Athena and says, "Let me help."

Athena looks at the angel, disregarding a dying angel, while they hear screech after screech. The dying angel touches her feet, and she feels an amplifying surge as she looks down and sees the angel touching her. She looks at him, confused, as the angel says, "I can amplify your strikes, just get me up." Athena looks as she hears a bellow from the dome, "Stay down."

Poseidon, watching the angel, moves to pick him up and hold him up as the silver blood drip out of his nose as another screech comes from the dome.

The dying angel says, "Give me a few minutes to charge you."

Athena's vines begin to glow silver as she feels wave after wave of pure energy fill her. Her eyes begin to shoot sparks she hears a woman scream in the dome, fuelling her even more as the angel says, "A couple of more seconds." Athena's vines begin shooting sparks as her skin begins to tear. She screams, releasing a bolt of lightning that powers through the ice and sends a booming thunder as the angel falls. She looks and sees Violence carrying Wrath out of a crack of the ice toward them, his eyes burning with rage.

The ice falls as the Hydra's head is seared off by Athena's bolt. The other heads break free from the weakened walls and look at the missing head as they look at the group.

Violence stares back as he says in a low voice, "We burn the heads off."

Athena looks at Violence as she breathes in, energizing herself, as Poseidon and Violence charge at the beast. One head snaps at Violence. He grabs the head and throws it in the dirt as the other head comes to help. It is met with a trident to the nose as Athena lets loose a bolt, searing the head that Violence was holding down. Violence throws the head and looks at the last one as it entangles with Poseidon. Violence summons his chain and throws it around the Hydra's neck and pulls. As the chain grips the neck, it lets loose a crimson burst, yanking the Hydra's head down as Athena lets loose another bolt. The head falls and flops on the ground, as Violence looks at it curiously.

Athena walks up behind him and says, "It is immoral."

Violence looks at it and asks, "Why this one though?"

Athena responds, "This was the main head."

Violence slams his fist down on it, cracking its eye, as Athena stares at disbelief toward Violence's actions. She tries to restrain him as she whispers, "Go be with Aphrodite, brother."

That catches his attention as he kicks the head one last time and turns around to see Wrath standing with no wound on her. He looks at her puzzled as she stares back at him as she says, "The angel took his life and saved mine."

Violence goes to her and holds her, thankful she is still with him.

She pushes him away little as he pulls her back in.

She says, "Never crush my hand again."

Violence responds, "Never try to sacrifice yourself for me again."

She sighs and enjoys his embrace as her eyes go back to a rainbow color, feeling like herself again.

Poseidon walks up to them, and as Violence and Wrath see him as, he says, "Father, Mother."

Violence looks at him and grabs him, then pulls him in as he says, "Son."

Wrath holds him to as she says, "My darling boy, Phobos."

Phobos lets them go as Violence asks, "How are you enjoying your new position?"

Phobos responds, "It's nothing new. The ocean is full of anxiety and fear."

Athena walks over as she says, "Nephew."

Phobos looks at her, confused, as he asks his father, "Are you two on speaking terms again?"

Violence looks at Athena, then says, "For now."

Phobos shakes it off and says to all of them, "Ares is on this earth as she has with her the last angel."

Wrath looks even more on edge as she says, "Why does she not show herself, son?"

Phobos stares at the ground, thinking of how to word it, as he says, "It is her nature."

Violence looks at Wrath and then says, "Our daughter always knew how to start drama."

Athena smirks as she says, "The only one not invited to our father's wedding out of fear."

Phobos looks at her in disgust as Violence says to him, "There is no harm in telling the truth, son."

Photo relinquishes the gaze as a helicopter comes down; and a group of soldiers, fully armed, files in followed by Aten.

Lucifer looks at a small crystal ball and sees everything unfolding. He smiles at the ball, slowly getting up off his obsidian throne and begins to walk to a door at the end of a room. He walks through the door to violence realm and sees the imp carrying body parts around to his tiny throne that Ares made for him. Lucifer walks up to the imp startling the imp, "My overlord master forgive me, I did not know you were here." Lucifer holds his hand out to stop him from talking as he begins speak, "Do you have imp" the Imp looks at him then scurries away and comes back with a vial of Ares crimson energy. The imp rolls it to Lucifer squeaking "As commanded" Lucifer makes the ground beneath the vial rise. He takes it in his hands and stares at it. He opens his bag with other essence from the different angels. Lucifer can feel the imp curiosity muttering to the imp "I can not tell you much, just know this will grow." Lucifer walks away thru the door.

14

Aten looks over everybody, and he sees a new face. Then he realizes one face is missing as he looks around to find Limbo. Athena walks up to him as she says, "We had a traitor among us."

Aten looks at Violence and Wrath as they begin to move to him broken and tired as he nods and motions everyone to fall back. Violence is hovering over Wrath as Heresy escorts them.

Wrath looks at Violence as she says sweetly, "I am fine, I can walk."

Violence looks at her as he says sternly, "What if the venom comes back?"

Wrath looks at him with tender eyes as she says, "I'll explain everything, but right now, trust me."

Violence backs off a little as Heresy looks at his father with doubt. Heresy gets closer to his mother as Wrath tells Heresy "I am fine, my son."

Heresy nods as he puts his weapon away and walks to the helicopter. Athena is already there and ready to leave. The rest of the group get to Athena. Athena extends her hand to help Wrath up as Wrath looks at the gesture. She takes it as an olive branch. Heresy looks at his father again, confused, as Violence shrugs at him as to say, "Get on the helicopter and fly back to base."

The ride is quiet as everyone has question, but now is not the time.

They get back to base. As the soldiers start unloading the gear, Violence looks at them with pity.

Wrath notices his demeanor and asks, "What is it?"

Violence sighs as he says somberly, "They were willing to sacrifice themselves for us, knowing that they cannot help."

Wrath grabs his arm as she says calmly, "They believe in us and are willing to defend their home with nothing but hope and bravery."

Violence lets Wrath pull him away as they walk into the mission control room.

Aten takes a seat as he says, "All right, where to begin?"

Violence looks up and says defeated, "Our brother has betrayed us."

Aten sighs as he asks, "Why?"

Athena speaks up. "He wants more than what he has already. They believe they are entitled to more."

Aten looks at Athena as he says, "None of you angel are entitled to anything. Ever since you have entered the world, it has been one thing after another."

Heresy looks at him with rage.

Aten notices, and he puts his hand on his side, ready to draw his weapon.

Heresy speaks up. "I do not know you, mortal, but I can tell you right now that humanity as a whole has always had one thing after another. As we give life, you take life."

Aten looks at him with gall as he raises his voice. "We are the rightful owners of this world."

Heresy replies, "You are not the rightful owner of anything but your soul and only your soul. I have seen your kind mess with forces you know nothing about, just trying to another leg up on each other. If we left humanity alone, you would be gone in ten years max, from nukes to greed. You have no idea what you are doing. So stand down, Aten, as we are your only hope that you have a place to live and breathe in your lungs."

Aten thinks as he sees the truth in Heresy's words. He relaxes and states, "So what now?"

Wrath looks around as she comes with an idea. She holds her hand up and says, "We need to see Alexander. He will know where the next step lies."

Violence smiles an evil smile as Athena shakes her head in disbelief. She attempts to protest, "There has to be another way to get information."

Wrath sighs as she says, "I am out of ideas. We need to have a plan, not just reacting to what is happening."

Athena hangs her head down low as Aten looks at them, confused, then he asks, "Who is Alexander?"

Violence answers him with eagerness, "The Great."

Aten looks even more confused as he says, "The Great?"

Wrath answers Aten, "Alexander the Great."

Aten looks even more confused as he's says, "That person died hundreds of years ago."

Violence smiles as he says, "He did die, but we made a deal as he called out to me before he died."

Aten gives up as he says, "I have no clue what is happening."

Violence replies, "The story is he died, but we made a deal he if rules over Atlantis."

The doctor looks up with enthusiasm as he says, "Atlantis? As in the lost city?"

Violence smiles as he gets up and moves to the doctor to massage his back as he tells him, "The city was never lost. They were just too strong of a civilization that they asked God to hide the city so they may not lose their progress."

The doctor writes in his notebook, trying to capture every word.

Violence continues as he whispers, "They asked to be cured of the rest of the imbeciles of this world."

The doctor turns his head and looks at Violence in his eyes as he asks, "They wanted to be quarantined from the world as if we were the infection."

Heresy speaks up. "It was not as dramatic as my father is making it out to be, but in essence, yes. They were constantly under attack, so they prayed they had the most angelic metal, so the one true father granted them their seclusion."

Violence looks at his son as he says, "For they really hated the world." Violence moves back to his chair.

The doctor straightens himself up and says, "How much more advanced can they be? We have world-ending technology."

Wrath responds, "They had before the new world was even found. They have even found cures to illness that don't even occupy their own living."

Aten sighs and says, "What is the point of this conversation? Can we get back on topic?"

Violence takes his seat as he says, "We need to go there."

Aten looks at Wrath for a second opinion. Wrath stares back, defeated. Then he looks at Athena as his last hope as she looks down. Aten looks at Violence.

He sits smiling a creepy smile.

He eventually asks, "Why are you smiling?"

Violence responds, "Because we need a blood of sacrifice of three men."

Aten looks at him and says, "What?"

Violence responds, "We need enough blood of three men."

Aten looks at Violence and sighs as he says, "I'll need time to think about it. However, I need to make transportation, and I do not have an idea where."

Athena responds, "The lost city is in the depths of Bermuda Triangle."

Violence responds, "Hurry now, Director. Time is ticking, and our enemies are formidable."

The angels get up and leave for a much needed rest. Wrath follows Violence to the rec room as they take a seat. Violence is still smiling at the choices that the director will have to make.

Wrath breaks his concentration as she asks, "Why did you keep the ring?"

Violence's smile quickly goes away as responsibility brings him back to reality. He sighs, then responds, "Are we really going to do this now?"

Wrath looks determined to get to the bottom of it.

Violence sees her determination as he continues, "The reason why I kept it is because it reminded me of happiness, something very valuable in the hells."

Wrath smiles as she is satisfied, then she moves a pillow to his lap and lies on his lap. Violence's eyes go back to being gold. Wrath's eyes go back to her natural rainbow color as she looks up at Violence.

Violence looks down and proceeds to ask her, "Why did you?"

Wrath smiles and says, "Even in death, you will still be mine. Tell me what you told me when you proposed."

Violence looks annoyed but can't help but to smile at her as he says, "I would recognize you in total darkness, were you mute and I deaf. I would recognize you in another lifetime entirely in different bodies, different times. And I would love you in all of this until the very last star in the sky burned out into oblivion."

Wrath smiles as she says, "It sounds just as good when you first said it as Achilles."

Violence rubs her head as he says, "I am quite the charmer when I want to be."

Wrath sighs and gets up. As he looks confused, she says, "Of course, you would kill the mood."

Violence gently grabs her by the hips and playfully pulls her back down as she laughs and smiles. She returns back to her resting spot. She thinks of the last time she felt this safe, then she falls asleep. He stares at her as she sleeps and thinks back to their house and of them raising of their kids. He thinks back to their training. As he thinks, he remembers the one that failed. He starts to think harder as Athena and Heresy walks in the room squabbling.

Wrath wakes up, and she looks at them.

Athena sees both of their eyes and proceeds, "Can you tell your son to stop preaching to me about the absence of justice if there is bravery."

Violence looks at both of them as his eyes comes back to a crimson color. Wrath gets up, allowing Violence to stand up. Violence stands up, and he looks at both of them in disappointment. He says, "Are you imbeciles playing a typical joke right now?"

They both looks at Violence in disbelief.

Violence reads the room and continues, "We have world-ending problems, and you are arguing over justice right now. Heresy, I expected more from you. We cannot help those who do not want to hear our truth. Athena, you are arguing with clearly a child still. I never thought I would be the one talking reason to you, but I need you both to come to sense."

Athena and Heresy looks at each other.

Heresy sighs and whispers, "Truce?"

Athena looks at Heresy and nods.

Violence looks at both of them and says, "Now leave us until tomorrow. We shall discuss more."

Athena looks annoyed at taking orders, but she can hear the reason behind it as she begrudgingly abides to the order.

Heresy says, "Yes, Father, till tomorrow."

They both leave as Wrath stays, lying down, looking at Violence with here rainbow eyes and smiles.

Violence looks annoyed as he mutters, "What is it?"

Wrath talks through her smile, "That's the Ares I remember, the father of many of our children."

Violence picks her up as she squeals in excitement as he sits back down on the couch with her in his arms. Wrath hold on to him as she begins to relax and hears him says, "I never thought I would have to tell other angels how to act."

The doctor burst through the door and seems them as he stammers, "I-I need to know how much blood you need."

Violence sighs as Wrath sits up to handle the outburst. She calmly says, "Enough for three men."

The doctor nods and leaves as they get settled back.

She laughs and says, "We best get some sleep. "Violence sighs again as Wrath gently touches his face as she says, "Come find me in the darkness of sleep." Wrath gets up and walks away as Violence follows suit, back to his bunk.

15

The next day comes rather quickly as Wrath wakes up and throws on her clothes. She opens her door, and she sees Violence walking past her, holding up a coffee while drinking an energy drink.

She takes the coffee, confused, as he says, "They didn't have almond, so I got hazelnut."

Wrath looks even more confused as she asks, "How did you know?"

Violence smirks as he says, "Everyone is a creature of habit. Take my sister for an example. She will walk out yawning, and she will try to crack her back when she walks out."

He looks at his watch and holds his hand with his finger up, counting down.

She looks at him, confused.

As he reaches zero, she opens up her door and does as Violence predicted.

Athena sees them looking her and looks at them confused as she walks away.

Wrath turns and looks at Violence and asks, "How long have you been watching?"

Violence responds, "Let's be honest here. When we all showed up here, we weren't on the best of terms, so I look for the advantage. Even your fighting style has some gaps as does my sister. She still fights in a triangle motion. She chooses defense over offense."

Wrath looks at him in a disturbed look as she begins to realize he has a center to every angel here. She tries to level the playing ground and asks, "So what is your style?"

Violence can sense her discomfort as he responds, "My counter is getting me to rage, if that is the real question."

Wrath looks at him shock as this is a new part that she never noticed about him. After all this time, she is surprised by him.

He hears the intercom come on as Aten request the angels to the war room. He looks at her and cheers her with his C4 energy drink as he walks to the room.

Heresy comes up behind her and says, "Well, clearly, Dad is a lot more clever than we believed."

Wrath, startled by unexpected voice, jumps a bit as she yelps, "Can everyone just act normal for once?"

Heresy looks at her, confused, as he says, "If anyone needs their wits about them, it is you my dear mother."

Wrath realizes that she has let her guard down for Violence unconsciously. She nods to Heresy as they walk to the room.

They walk into the room as Aten stands in front of the table waiting for the rest of the group to get settled in.

Aten gets everyone's attention and begins by saying, "We have a carrier on the border of the Bermuda ready to do as requested."

Violence looks with anticipation as he asks, "Where are the sacrifices?"

Aten clears his throat as he replies, "The package is on the carrier."

Violence can sense something is off, but he lets it go.

Aten continues, "We have a plane ready to get you there, so mount up."

They get up as Aten states, "Violence...Wrath, please pause a moment before you leave."

Violence and Wrath stay sitting as Athena looks at them with suspicion as she leaves. Heresy looks to them worried as Violence waves him off not to worry. He leaves with Athena as Aten waits for the door to close and waves in the doctor.

Violence finally questions, "What is this about? We have a job to do."

Aten smiles and holds out a paper, then he slides it to them.

Violence and Wrath looks at the deed to an island off the Bahamas. Aten smiles as he says, "The senator came through on his word."

Wrath looks at Violence, confused, as she asks, "Who is the senator?"

Violence smirks and replies, "Someone who just gave us land for us to be together till we our bodies give out and we have to return to hell."

Wrath smiles as she looks at Violence with joy in her eyes while she says. "You have been planning this."

Violence replies, "I have planned a lot for us."

Wrath, unable to resist, reaches over her chair and hugs Violence as their eyes go back to their original colors.

Violence hugs her back as he whispers, "Let's finish this so we can enjoy the rest of this mortal life together."

She smiles and nods as they stand up and move to the hangar.

As they leave the door, Wrath looks at Violence and says, "The rest are coming too, right?"

Violence looks annoyed as he answers begrudgingly, "If they must."

Wrath gets even more excited as she jumps on Violence. Violence catches her and carries her till they get to hangar.

They walk through the door of the hangar, and Athena sees her brother's natural eyes color. She smiles, knowing they just received good news. Heresy begins to feel anxiety as he looks at his father, waiting to know the news.

Violence looks at his son as he says, "Still your nerves, Phobos. Nothing but good news my son."

Heresy calms down after hearing his name and makes his way to the armory to inspect the weaponry of the modern age.

They see a plane engine get started as the pilot calls them over. They get in and find a seat as the plane takes off. Violence and Wrath can feel a sudden dark pull to something. They both look at each other, both knowing something is going on.

—m—

Meanwhile, Limbo and Gluttony are sitting in a dark cave around a fire. They both look at each other, unsure about their choice.

Atlas walks into the cave hauling a dead dear and sets it down. He says, "We have nutrition for the night. As the air gets cold, the fire goes out."

A shadow figure comes out. As they look at it, they hear a voice.

"Why do you chase power?"

Atlas stares down the figure, trying to find out who it is. He thinks, *Treachery.* Atlas moves to the shadow as he answers the question that the shadow asked.

"I do not seek power, I seek my family."

The shadow begins to come in focus. It is a dark-haired woman.

Limbo states, "Ares?"

The lady turns to him as she says, "Well, if it isn't my cousin."

Limbo looks at Atlas as he can sense the question coming. He says, "This is Ares, Aphrodite's daughter."

Atlas says stoically, "We have met before. One question, why are you here?"

Ares turns to Atlas and replies, "Because you need my help, and I need your help to reach my own goals."

Atlas responds, "What are your goals?"

Ares responds, "My goals are my own. However, I can put your opposition into turmoil, giving you an advantage."

Atlas looks at her unconvinced as he says, "And how would you do that, angelic spawn?"

Ares looks at him with confidence as she begins to explain.

"I will make them fight each other as they have bad blood they are forgetting about. I will make them forget their main enemy."

Atlas responds, "What makes you think I need your help?"

Ares responds, confused, "They killed a Hydra without suffering any casualties. They took an immortal war machine designed to keep bigger things than Titans outside of the gates of heaven."

Atlas stares, looking convinced, as she continues, "However, you make them fight each other, and they are guaranteed to suffer casualties, giving you time uninterrupted by them."

Atlas sits down confidently as he says, "How would you do that?"

Ares smiles as she says, "I will try to make them a deal and bring up old wounds that will make them argue with each other."

Gluttony thinks for a moment as he says, "This could work, if she can get Ares and Aphrodite to fight, Athena will join Aphrodite to have number, just to prove a point to Ares."

Ares smiles as she says, "There is only thing that I need from you, Atlas."

Atlas looks at her, waiting for her to say what she wants.

She continues, "I am going to offer a deal on your behalf. If they accept, you have to make good on the deal."

Atlas responds, "What deal would that be?"

Ares looks at Limbo as she says, "Ares will want power and refuge. We offer it, and they will fight. However, the off chance they do take the deal, we will have to make good on it, or you will become their main enemy again."

Limbo breaks his silence and says, "This could be a good thing to have. Ares is an animal that can break wills."

Atlas smiles as he stands up and holds his right hand out. Ares takes it and shakes on it. As they shake on it, a black shock wave emits.

Atlas asks, "What was that?"

Ares responds to the question, "Whenever I make a deal, it does that."

—∞—

Violence and the group get off the plane that has landed on a carrier. They are greeted by an admiral.

"Hey, we had word that you guys were coming. Follow me and I'll lead you to the buggy."

They follow him, and he begins to ask questions.

"I heard you guys were different."

Violence responds, "You could say that."

The admiral continues, "What is your mission over here?"

Wrath responds, "That is not up for discussion."

The admiral smiles. "Can't blame me for trying."

Athena responds, "How long have you been in ocean?"

The admiral responds, "Since I could talk. My family were fishers, and I chose a similar but much different path."

151

Heresy responds, "Have you seen any weird creatures in these beautiful waters?"

The admiral responds, "Everything is weird in the ocean. I can swear on my life I have seen a megalodon awhile back, but no one believes me."

Heresy smiles as he responds, "They do exist. You are fortunate to be alive if you have encountered one."

The admiral responds, "That is very true, my friend. That thing is longer than some submarines."

Violence glares at Heresy, knowing he created an ocean monster again. Heresy can feel the cold dagger stares from his father as they reach a little boat.

The admiral turns around and says, "Here is the chariot, my friends, and the package is inside."

Violence looks and sees a little cooler. He turns to him and says in a low growl, "What is this?"

The admiral shrugs his shoulder and says, "It was dropped off late last night, and I was instructed not to open it."

Athena smiles as she says, "They are more clever than they lead on."

The admiral says, "Godspeed," as he turns and leaves.

Wrath can't help but to smile as Violence opens the case and sees nothing but pints of blood in there."

Violence growls, "They will suffer for this. Leave it up to humans to take the fun out of a ritual."

Athena retorts, "This way, no one has to die, and it fulfils the cost of entry."

Violence takes a seat on the buggy, pouting. The rest of the group takes a seat as they are lowered in the water. They start the engine as Heresy takes over the steering. As they get closer, the electronics start to go out as the compass begins to go back and forth. The engine cuts out as Heresy summons his trident and gently lowers it in the ocean. The boat begins to move forward, powered by the waves as Violence looks underneath. He can see a bunch of fish pushing the boat to a small rock island in the middle of the ocean.

Heresy docks it. As they get up of the buggy and look around on the ground, they see a little hole in the ground in the shape of a spear head. Heresy looks at it as he tries to figure it out.

Athena walks over, confused as well, as she says, "What is this?"

Violence grabs the container and stacks the blood on top of each other as he summons a spear and slams it in the hole as the blood feeds down the tip of the spear. They wait as nothing happens.

Athena lets out a sigh as she begins to doubt. She says, "Looks like you were—"

She is cut off by the ground clicking. The rock begins to crack open as the ground starts to lower into the depths of the ocean. An air bubble forms around them as they get deeper and darker. They see a city under the ground as the lights breaks the darkness. The small ground hits the ground, and the bubble shatters, but the water is contained on the outside as they catch their grounding.

16

The group lands in a glowing blue liquid that is cooling to the touch. The rest of the group gather their footing. As they step into the liquid, they are met by a group of men that are armed with their combat gear.

Violence looks at them and their weaponry as he sizes them up if things go wrong.

Athena states, "We do not come to cause harm, Atlanteans."

The Atlanteans stand their ground as they hear footstep of an older man.

One of the Atlanteans state, "The Great shall decide your intentions."

The shadow grows bigger as the old man takes his time to come around the corner.

Violence grows impatient as he says, "Hurry up, you're old as it is. It not like you got much longer to live."

An old voice comes around the corner. "I cannot die thanks to you, Ares."

Wrath looks at Violence in confusion as Violence looks irritated by the response.

The old man walks around the corner in a robe showing a scar in the middle of stomach with his eyes glowing bright blue, the same as the liquid beneath their feet.

Violence looks at the old man as he says, "I didn't think you are still alive, Alexander."

Alexander responds coldly, "You know I cannot die. I regret our deal as I will never know the sweet release of death."

Violence responds sharply, "Two things. One is, you are the one that decided to commit suicide and reach out to me again, and second, how did you know it was me?"

Alexander holds a device in his hand and presses it. It shows a map and where every angel is. Alexander puts it away and responds, "I fought many wars, expanding the Black Wolf legacy known as Rome. But everlasting life is not something I would have ever wish on my greatest enemies."

Violence cracks his neck as he says, "Help me recall what is it you asked me to do when you called for me on the ground as your sword was puncturing your stomach."

Alexander looks at him and sighs, then says, "I asked to not die here."

Violence responds to that. "I held up my deal, my great one."

Alexander chuckles as he says, "I was not the great one. You had your favorite through the times."

Violence looks at him in disbelief as he says, "How many battles you should have lost, but I favored you and lent you a fraction of my strength."

Alexander is getting annoyed as he says, "Tell me what you want, Ares."

Violence responds quickly, "I want that thing in your hand."

Alexander looks at him and says, "I never knew you to be the type to hunt other angels, maybe demons."

Athena breaks her silence as she says, "A Titan is on the earth, and he is trying to release the other Titans."

Alexander takes a seat as he ponders.

Athena continues, "We can handle the problem. However, we need to find them. You need not fret."

Alexander looks at Athena as he responds to her, "I am not afraid of death, I welcome it." He pauses for a moment as he says, "Are you Athena?"

Athena nods her head as Alexander looks confused to see Ares and Athena in the same room together. Alexander chuckles again as he says,

"Time must truly be desperate considering you are not fighting each other. I must admit it is somewhat unusual." Alexander thinks and says, "We can make a deal, Ares. I will give you this, and you kill the beast a shadow dropped in our mines."

Violence looks at him and says, "Or I could just cut off your arm."

Athena chimes in, "We are not doing that, brother. We can be diplomatic."

Alexander smiles as he responds to Violence, "You could, no doubt in my mind that you can best an old legend. However, it requires an energy source that I only know where it is."

Violence looks even more annoyed as he says, "Then show me to the beast, and let's be done with it."

Alexander smiles as he gets up and begins to walk, the guard following him. He walks very slow, and the group feels annoyed at the speed he is moving at. The Atlanteans honor his walking speed by slowing down.

Violence sighs as he says, "Are you handicapped now?"

Wrath elbows his arm as to be patient.

Alexander answers, "My body is barely holding on to the sands of time."

Violence's hand glows a crimson red as he places his hand on Alexander's back and the crimson flows through his body. He begins to get younger as his body begins to crack. He falls to the ground, and the Atlantean guards begin to ready for battle. Alexander holds his hand up, telling them to halt as he tries to stand up. The guard tries to help him up. Alexander pushes him away as he stands straight up and looks at Violence with wonder.

Alexander asks curiously, "What did you just do to me?"

Violence responds confidently, "I gave you some of your youth back. Your cells were degenerating and not rejuvenating, so I gave you some more at the cost of this mortal life suit."

Alexander moves his legs up and down, then does a little jump. As he lands, he begins to smile.

Athena can't help but to smile as her brother finally did something nice for his warriors.

Violence breaks the mood as he says, "Can we get a move on now?"

Wrath smacks him again as Alexander turns to him, then says, "Of course, my dear friend."

Violence looks at him confused, then says, "Let's not get ahead of ourselves now."

Alexander mood cannot be broken as he walks tall and confident. They get to a waterfall, and he turns around and says, "Only two of you may enter this mine. There is not enough room for more."

Wrath holds on to Violence's arm, getting ready for the encounter about to come.

Alexander continues, "We are not sure what it is. However, it has destroyed team after team that we have sent in to get rid of the beast."

Athena looks at Wrath as she stares back, then he says, "Let me and Violence handle this one."

Wrath looks at her, untrusting, as she says, "Not a chance in hell."

Violence looks at Athena as she says, "It is better odds, Wrath. I'm not trying to imply you are not strong, but mine and Violence's power complement each other."

Wrath looks back at Violence as he stares in to her eyes. His eyes turn gold as he says, "I will not lose you again. My sister is disposable to me."

Athena snarks back, "Love you too, brother."

Wrath looks at Athena as she says, "Please, I know we haven't been on best terms but bring him back with his shield or on it."

Athena takes a moment to see the plea in her eyes as she nods her head.

Alexander tells the rest, "Wrath and Heresy, we can wait in the lounge." He points to the guards to lead them to it.

Violence watches Wrath walk away as Athena snaps her fingers in front of her brother's face. He breaks his stare as he looks at her. She looks at him in disgust and groans.

He smiles as he says, "I am only human."

Athena retorts, "Sometimes you remind me of our father."

Violence smiles at his sister as he says, "Sometimes you remind me of mother."

Athena smiles as she says, "That is probably one of the nicest things you ever said to me."

Violence responds, "Do not look at my words, look at my actions, dear sister." He moves closer to her as he picks up her hand and holds it up, showing her forearm brace. Violence says, "Do you remember when I gifted you this?"

Athena responds, "I do. I just accidentally killed Pallas. May she rest in peace."

Violence lets her hand go and picks up his hand and shows a similar brace as he says, "This wasn't meant to be a trophy for your kill. This was meant to be a symbol of how our father has scarred us both, and in the end we are still brother and sister."

Athena thinks on it as she says, "I never thought of it like that, brother."

Violence responds, "I never spoken openly about it. You know who skewed that fight?"

Athena nods her head as she begins to tear up a bit, then she says, "I miss her, brother."

Violence stands in solace as he says, "I know, my dear sister. I know it's part of the reason why you try to choose peace over warfare."

Athena stands in silence as she is surprised that her brother was being vigilant on his rationing and thought process.

Violence breaks the silence as he says, "Anyways, this is a lovely talk, but we have a beast to kill."

—❧—

Wrath makes her way into the lounge as she sees more Atlanteans relaxing as they unload their gear and make their way to bar. A guard hops behind the bar and starts making drinks.

Heresy looks at his mother and says, "I want to part take in this."

Wrath stops him as she says, "What if your father needs you?"

Heresy responds, "Then he shall see Thor reincarnate." He laughs and makes his way to bar.

Wrath follows her son as they have two bright blue drinks dropped off in front of them. Heresy picks it up and holds it up as the Atlanteans watch and cautiously raise their glasses, cheering.

Heresy and Wrath drink the blue drinks. The drink tastes like the clearest water they have ever had followed by a slow burn.

Heresy gulps it in as he asks, "What is this?"

The guard playing bartender responds, "We call it the Juice."

Heresy retorts, "What is in it? It is unusual to me."

The guard laughs as he says, "It is fermented kiwi mixed with our water."

Wrath looks at her empty glass, and the bartender fills them both back up to fullest.

One of the beefy guards stares at Heresy. He can feel it, and he turns to him and asks, "What is wrong?"

The guard looks at him and responds, "I've never seen an angel so close. Do you bleed?"

Heresy smiles as he says with a devil's charm. "I do, however, I can show you strength in other ways if you are interested."

The guard stands up, and he towers over Heresy. He says, "What did you have in mind?"

Heresy finds a little table and clears it off. He takes a seat and holds his hand to the other chair as the guard takes a seat. The guard takes a seat, and Heresy places his elbow on the table and prepares for an arm wrestle. The guard can't help but to smile as a friendly competition arises.

—w—

Athena and Violence enter a small dark crack in the wall as they squeeze through. The only light illuminating the way are small water balls still glowing bright blue.

Violence whispers, "Why is this so tiny? Who is mining down here?"

Athena turns her head and looks at him in a scolding manner as she continues to move through the cave till the reach a small room. They look around, and they cannot see anything that would harm them. The only thing they see is broken rocks and blue lights. Violence and Athena look at each other in confusion. Athena takes a couple steps forward and sees broken bones picked clean. Athena clicks her tongue to get Violence's attention. He hears the click, then turns to her and sees her pointing at the bones. He moves to her and examines it, trying to discover what beast they are dealing with. Violence clicks his tongue to Athena as he points to his shoulder. She sees his signal, then slowly moves to him and places her hand on his shoulder. He feels Athena's hand and slowly crouches to the ground and places his hand on the floor as he pulses the cave. They see a heartbeat and a sleeping wolf's head that is abnormally big.

Athena lets his shoulder go as Violence stands up and says, "They lost to an overgrown Pomeranian?"

Athena looks puzzled as she says, "There has to be more to this."

Violence smugly says, "Please do not over think the obvious, sister." He begins to walk confidently into the beast's den as Athena follows.

They reach the beast as the beast's nostrils take in the air. The beast can smell their presence as it begins to wake up. Violence sees it head move as it starts to release part of another head. Violence backs up a bit, realizing he is dealing with Cerberus. Athena sees Violence stepping back as she moves forward to see what is making her brother unsettled. Athena sees Cerberus come to life as it stands up.

Waking up, Cerberus sees intruders and can smell the sulfur coming off them. He begins to growl a low bellow.

Violence nervously says, "Who is a good boy?"

Cerberus heads begins to snarl at Violence.

Violence hands begin to glow crimson as he summons a shield and his kopis.

Athena gets behind Violence as she summons her sword.

Cerberus barks as it begins to grow bigger, now towering over them.

Athena says to Violence, "Why would you wake that thing up?"

Violence responds, "Now is not the time, sister."

Cerberus snaps at Violence as his shield takes the blow but pushing him back from sheer strength. Athena presses Violence back, giving him reinforcement from Cerberus's strength. Athena responds to Cerberus's snap by throwing a lightning bolt at it. As it makes contact on its back, the sound of thunder follows as Cerberus yelps in pain. The left head of Cerberus snaps over the top of the shield, barely missing Athena. Cerberus dashes toward them as Violence swings his sword downward, cutting the nose of Cerberus as it barks. Rocks vibrate off the cave and starts falling on them. One rock hits Violence's head making him recoil. He lowers his guard as Cerberus stomps his paw on Violence, pinning him down. The claws press on the shield, making it crack. Athena lets loose a massive thunderbolt on Cerberus. As it hits, the thunder shakes the rocks again, this time landing on Cerberus's paw. It recoils, letting go of Violence, allowing him to get back up.

Violence stands back and commands Athena, "Use your fog!"

Athena looks at him in confusion, but the air starts to condense as the fog starts to cloud the room, blinding everyone in the cave. Cerberus tries to smell where they are, but all he can smell is the water in the air. It starts to back up to the wall, still growling. Violence pulses the ground and finds Athena. He runs to her and grabs her hand and puts it on his shoulder. She feels a sudden grab as she recoils in fear, but the hand leads to a shoulder. Violence crouches again as he pulses the room, and she sees Cerberus back in a corner, scared and confused. Violence grips her hand hard. As she feels it, she begins to brace herself for what Violence is planning on. As she feels him pulls her hard, she is launched at Cerberus. As she slams, her hand pommel on the middle head, leaving Cerberus dazed. Violence charges with his shield on the left head, right behind Athena. He hears a yelp as he slashes his sword at the right head, clipping its lip. The Cerberus begins to cower in fear.

Athena pushes Violence away, knocking him back.

He stares in confusion. He stares her down as he says, "What?"

Athena looks at Cerberus as it cowers, and she says in a low tone, "He knows he is defeated."

Violence cautiously walks toward it as the heads back up against the cave wall. Violence sighs as he lowers his guard as he says, "Now what?"

Athena thinks for a moment as she walks up to Cerberus. As she approaches Cerberus, it snaps to defend itself as it stares. One of the heads stares at Athena's weapons. Athena sets it down as Cerberus begins to calm down. As she approaches, she holds her hands up as it tries to back further in a corner. She touches it gently. It starts to relax. She feels its heartbeat as it slowly begins to slow down. As the heart rate begins to slow down, the size of Cerberus begins to get smaller as it starts to trust Athena. One of the heads looks at Violence as it begins to slowly move to Violence.

Athena says to Violence, "Put down your weapons."

Violence looks at her unsure as Athena pleads with her eyes. He slowly lowers his weapons as Cerberus smells Violence's legs. Violence looks at the three-headed dog. Cerberus, unsure, begins to slowly wag his tail as he licks Violence's feet. As slobber get on his boot, Violence groans. Cerberus begins to wag his tail faster. Hearing Violence make a noise, he starts to lick Violence's face as Violence says, "Back you, furry beast." Cerberus continues to lick as Violence snaps his fingers as he points down. Cerberus sits down, wagging his tail as the other heads stare at Violence as their new master.

Violence looks at Athena for guidance as Athena laughs as she says, "He likes you." Athena uses her puppy voice as she says, "Come here, big boy."

One of the heads turns to look at her as the other ones stay fixed on Violence. She begins to look disappointed. Violence snaps and points to Athena as Cerberus gets up and sits on Athena's feet, staring at Violence. As Cerberus sits on Athena's foot, the weight of Cerberus makes Athena groan in pain.

Violence says, "Good boy."

Cerberus starts to wag his tail faster as it whips Athena's legs. Athena rubs Cerberus stomach as she endures the pain as the happy dog as looks in plea to Violence. Violence eventually gives in as he motions his hand to Cerberus to follow. Cerberus gets up and walks to Violence as one of the heads try to lick Violence's legs again. Violence snaps his legs as the heads looks up at Violence. As he signals to follow, Cerberus follows.

Athena looks at him confused as she asks, "What are you doing?"

Violence responds, "I am not killing anything that is loyal to me. That's your job."

Athena shakes her head as she follows the unlikely duo out of the cave.

Violence exits the cave entrance as the guard looks at Violence, surprised that he is still alive and not much damage has been done to him. As Cerberus follows and shows himself, the guard looks at beast in shock.

Violence sees the guard's looks, then says, "Lower your weapons. He is under control."

Cerberus sees the guard, and he starts to cower behind Violence for protection.

The guard looks uncertain but does as Violence commands. Violence nods in gratitude as he says, "Where are the rest?"

The guard stammers, staring at the beast behind Violence, "They... they are in the lounge with the others."

Athena finishes squeezing through. As she see Cerberus cowering behind Violence, she pats Cerberus, trying to get him to relax as he slowly wags his tail in appreciation. The guard looks even more shocked to see both of them come out almost unscathed. Violence stares at the guard to lead. The guard turns and starts to lead them to lounge.

As the walk closer, they hear cheering and cups being slammed on the table. Athena and Violence look at each other as they hear a table break. The guard and them quickly rush in to see Heresy and Wrath drinking and making bets on arm wrestling.

Wrath sees Violence and Cerberus, and she hurries over to them, skipping over Violence right to Cerberus. Cerberus is loving her touch and lies down and shows his belly, wagging his tail in delight.

Heresy walks over to him and says, "Come join us, Father."

Violence can smell the intoxication on his breath. Violence looks behind him and sees Wrath on the ground with Cerberus, snuggling him, as the three heads lick her face.

Athena walks over them and says, "Where is Alexander?"

The moment she says it, it like a ghost hearing its name in ages. He appears, making the guards snap to attention.

Alexander walks in and sees the Cerberus. He looks shocked to see what is beneath his city.

Violence walks to him and says, "The beast has been subdued."

Alexander responds to him. "I can see that."

Cerberus rubs his back on the ground as Wrath holds him.

Alexander looks in wonder as he has never laid eyes on the Cerberus. Alexander asks, "How did he get down there?"

Violence shrugs, just as confused as him. Violence thinks as he asks Alexander, "What is down there?"

Alexander sighs as he says, "Angel metal"

Violence looks at Alexander even more confused as he continues, "What is an angel metal doing down here?"

Alexander shrugs as he says, "God's gift to us, for us to continue his work."

Violence looks around and sees the structure.

Athena breaks her silence as she is eavesdropping. "This whole place is angel metal."

Alexander hands a device to Violence. Violence takes it and looks at it and can see where the traitors are. Violence looks at Alexander and nods.

Alexander nods back in respect. Alexander looks at Violence, then says, "Till next time, my old friend, feel free to use our portal to get back home."

Athena chimes in, "You have a portal?"

Alexander smiles as he says, "With the absence of intruders, it has allowed us to prosper without interference."

Violence turns and calls for Wrath. He sees Cerberus lying on Wrath now.

She says, intoxicated, "I am currently occupied."

Violence snaps his fingers, and Cerberus walks over to Violence as Wrath gets up.

Violence looks at the room and says, "Angels, we leave now."

Heresy slams one more drink and walks to the guard that got him started as he says, "Till next time, soldier."

The guard replies, "Next time I won't be so easy on you, tiny man."

Heresy smiles and walks over to the group as they turn to leave.

17

The group follows the guard to the portal.

As they reach the room, Athena turns to Violence, then says, "What is that contraption he gave you?"

Violence hands it over and says, "Keep it. I was already thinking about toying with it."

Wrath rolls her eyes as she says with liquor on her breath, "He could never leave things alone."

Violence ignores that comment as Athena examines it. As it turns on, she sees more dots on the world than expected. She examines it closely and finds them as they give off similar but different vibrations. Athena sees one vibration that looks just like Violence's energy, then it disappears. She looks at it, puzzled.

Violence sees her confusion. He asks her, "What is it?"

Athena straightens her look as she says, "There was another signature just like yours, but it has disappeared."

Violence doesn't look fazed as he says cockily, "Everyone wants to be like me."

Athena sees Wrath turn ghost white as she looks with uncertainty. Athena moves to her and says, "What do you know?"

Wrath regains her focus the question as she thinks, quickly sobering her up as she answers, "We were innocent."

Athena can sense a little lie in there, but she cannot figure out what the lie is.

Violence relaxes as he knows this is could be a volatile subject.

Athena thinks more as Wrath says, "You helped destroy my home."

Violence steps in as the guard looks confused as what is going but doesn't want to interfere. Violence looks at them and says, "Not here, not right now."

Athena and Wrath begrudgingly agree.

Cerberus senses Wrath's emotions, and he walks over and licks her hand to break her death stare.

The guard looks uneasy as Violence gives him the coordinates to the base. The guard works quickly to get out of an awkward situation, turning dials to the coordinates. The portal hums to life as it begins to gather water and glow a bright blue.

Violence looks at the guard and says, "Is everything you do down here have to do with water?"

The guard nods as he says, "We believe God's symbol is water, from the miracle of childbirth."

Violence holds his hand up to stop as he says, "Never mind, I am sorry I asked."

The guard looks offended as he presses on more buttons, and the portal opens. They walk through as they are on the landing strip of the base. They begin to walk as the soldier readies their arms, seeing them appear out of nowhere.

Aten comes out with his 1911 drawn. As he sees them, he gives the order, "Stand down, friendly."

The soldiers lower their weapons and go back to what they are doing at Aten's command. Aten puts his weapon back and approaches them. He sees the giant three-headed dog at Violence's side. He stares at it, unsure what to think.

Violence breaks his silence, then says, "This is Spot." He snaps his finger and motions to Cerberus to come forward. Cerberus three heads begins sniffing all the different parts of Aten.

Aten, nervous, pets Cerberus.

The doctor comes out full on sprinting as he sees Cerberus. He begins recording. He exclaims, "The guard dog of Hades. I can't believe it."

One of the heads of Cerberus looks at the doctor as to try to identify if he is a threat or friend.

Violence begins to get annoyed as he snaps to get Cerberus attention and points at the doctor. Cerberus charges at the doctor and pounces on him, licking his face until he starts laughing.

Violence looks at Aten and tiredly says, "We need to rest. We shall talk more about this in the morning."

Aten looks at him and can see that the long day has worn on him. He nods his head and says, "Till tomorrow then."

The group walks inside to get some much needed rest. Cerberus sees Violence and Wrath leaving. Cerberus follows him, leaving the doctor covered in slobber. Violence makes his way to the recreational hall as Wrath goes with him. Violence can feel Wrath wanting to explode about something. He can feel the tension of wanting to talk about something. He sits on the couch as Wrath lies on him again, and Cerberus lies down on the foot of the couch.

Violence rubs her head and says, "What is on your mind? You have been eerily quiet since the portal."

Wrath balls up and begins to quietly cry. Violence massages her head as she quietly cries on Violence's lap, trying to calm herself down. They sit there for a moment as she finally calms down enough to make one coherent sentence.

"We had our life stolen."

Violence sighs as he can't deny the truth. He calmly says, "Let's not focus on the past. We are here now."

Wrath looks at him, hurt, as she retorts, "Why are you so calm about this?"

Violence realizes his mistake as he tries to walk it back. "I am. However, I wanna be in the present with you right now."

Wrath continues to cry, not satisfied with Violence's reaction to having their life stolen. She stays silent, thinking that maybe this is what he wanted. *Did he want to leave?* She feels such emotion and falls asleep from emotional exhaustion.

Athena hears her crying and begins to feel guilty that she was so quick to rip her brother's life apart without hesitation in the name of justice. Athena walks away to her bed in shame.

Heresy sees a commotion going on as he heads to his bunk to sleep everything off.

Violence sits there exhausted, caught in the moment with Wrath as he feels anger but does not want to ruin the moment. He feels her fall fast asleep, then he picks her up and carries her to her room and tucks her in as Cerberus follow Violence. Violence gets ready to leave. Cerberus feels Wrath's pain and lies down next to her, looking to Violence to join. Violence looks down as he slowly closes the door and heads to his bunk with a mixture of emotions.

—m—

Atlas sits in their camp as they eat and prepare for their assault on the other angels. Limbo have the look of regret as he sighs.

Atlas recognizes the sigh. He looks at Limbo, then says in a mentoring manner, "Do not fret, angel. What we are doing is for the best."

Limbo looks at Atlas and chokes up, then nods his head in agreement.

Atlas notices the lie, and he continues, "I have been on this world before it was even green, when my family inhabited this place. There is no regret in doing what you think is best."

Limbo takes heed in his words and starts to relax.

A bright light appears, then Saint Michael appears out of the light. Limbo looks and gets a renewed hope, seeing his esteemed brother again. Limbo gets up and walks to his brother to embrace him as he says, "Brother, it is so good to see you again."

Saint Michael embraces his brother back in longing, but he couldn't help but notice the look in his eyes.

As they let each other go, Saint Michael asks Limbo "What is wrong, brother?"

Limbo responds to Saint Michael, "Just cold feet, that's it."

Saint Michael smiles and responds with charm, "Rebellion is never easy, brother."

Atlas walks over to Saint Michael sternly as he says, "We have almost secured the victory. There is one more angel with the horn."

Saint Michael retorts, "What is the hold up?"

Atlas looks at Saint Michael with disgust.

Saint Michael sees his looks he continues, "I meant nothing by the statement. We are in this together now."

Atlas lets it go and says, "I am planning for perfection, but this last angel is hiding somewhere protected."

Saint Michael sees a shadow move as he looks past Atlas, then he sees Ares. Saint Michael's eyes widen as he says, "What is she doing here?"

Atlas turns and sees Ares, and he responds, "Helping our cause."

Saint Michael moves past him to Ares and begins to question Ares. "What would make you move against your father?"

Ares responds, "My reasons are my own."

Saint Michael responds quickly and aggressively, "That's not an answer."

Ares stands up and says, "If you must know, when my father took Olympus by brutal strength with our help, his prize to me was for me to wed. While my brother received the trident and the seas, he would give me to another man."

Atlas intervenes as he says, "Stand down, it is in control."

Saint Michael takes a step back, letting him regain his self-control.

Atlas goes back to getting his gear ready. He looks to his left and sees Gluttony eating a bag of chips surrounded by empty bag of chip. Atlas sighs as he mutters to himself, "These are not warriors."

Saint Michael walks over to Atlas to examine how he is packing and is surprised to see almost nothing except a weapon and a little bit of food. Saint Michael voices his concern. "Why do you pack so little?"

Atlas stands up straight, then looks at Saint Michael as he says very somberly, "I never had anything to begin with, so I learned to work with little."

Saint Michael looks at Atlas and begins to feel guilty as he thinks to his own life and all of his privileges.

Atlas can see the sympathy as he continues, "I do not need your sympathy. This is what makes me stronger than most. When you have nothing, it your duty to make something."

Saint Michael sees the truth in the words and breaks his silence. "If you need me, call me..."

Atlas responds, "Actually, there is one thing I need you just to be aware of."

Saint Michael gives him his full attention.

Atlas continues, "I will try to recruit Ares."

Saint Michael looks like he has just seen a ghost as he says, "I will still kill him."

Atlas responds, "After the ritual, I do not have any care for what you do, as long it does not affect my cause."

Saint Michael nods as the bright light comes down again. He walks in and disappears with the light.

Atlas stands to his group and calls, "We move in the morning."

—◊◊◊—

The next morning arrives, and Wrath wakes up confused on how she ended up in her bed. She remembers Violence not being at all emotional on finding out their life was stolen. She begins to get angry again. As she sits up, her foot touches something furry. As she looks down, one of the three heads look up at Wrath, and Cerberus starts to wag his tail, seeing her awake. She reaches down and rubs the side of his belly as she maneuvers around him to get out of bed. She steps out and sees Athena with a guilty look on her face as she walks by, barely making any eye contact.

Athena continues to walk and sees her brother punching the punching bag while Heresy is doing pull-ups. Athena walks to cafeteria and gets the simple breakfast: eggs, sausage, and a biscuit. She sees Wrath walk in and go straight for the coffee machine with Cerberus following her around.

Wrath finishes her coffee as she pours three water bowls for Cerberus. They hear the alarm screech, and they instinctively move to the control room and see the doctor staring at a screen. They look at the screen and see Atlas and his group standing outside the base with several guards already dead.

Atlas senses he is being watched, and he looks at the camera. He motions his hand for them to come to him.

Violence summons his hellish gear as he begins to move.

Athena stops him by putting herself in the way, pleading "Brother, this is a trap. Can you not tell?"

Wrath starkly says, "She would know a thing about traps."

Violence looks at her, confused by her statement, but he shrugs it off and moves past Athena as they follow him outside.

Violence sees Atlas as he stops and think.

Atlas breaks the silence, "I have misjudged all of you so far. The Hydra was not an easy feat to accomplish."

Violence looks confused as he was anticipating a fight, but now hears compliments. It stuns him.

Atlas continues, "You were meant to be slaves, but during my time here, I have begun to see the potential in all of you. I will be merciful in offering all of you to join me in my mission for true paradise."

Athena looks at him, trying to decide if he is bluffing, but she can't see any that gives him away.

Atlas continues, "At least hear the offer before we make a mess of everything."

Athena speaks of the group. "Speak your peace then."

Atlas nods his head and proceeds to tell him about the offer. "Join me and all of you should ascend to Titans."

Athena looks at her brother and sees he is itching for battle. She looks at Wrath and sees her glaring at Violence, getting more and more irritated.

Violence can feel all the eyes. He sees a shadow slink away. As his eyes follow, he sighs and says, "Ares, my daughter, show yourself."

Wrath's face turns from anger to surprise to hear her daughter's name being called. As she looks around, a shadow appears in front of them.

Violence looks her over and says, "How are you, my daughter?"

Ares voice cracks as she says, "I am not your daughter, you animal."

Violence responds calmly, "It does not matter how far you go, how much you try to convince yourself that you aren't. My blood runs through your veins, oh daughter of mine."

The shadow becomes the figure of woman as she retorts, "I may have your blood but not your mistakes. You had the woman of your dreams, but you destroyed that."

171

Wrath looks at her daughter in pain as she continues, "You thought yourself better than your righteous sister and again you destroyed that."

Athena's eyes turn to Violence as Ares turns her gaze to her as she continues, "Tell me, Aunt, how many times did you have to bail your brother out just to have him fight you in return."

Athena stay silent but thinks about it as Violence smiles as he says, "That's why you are here, then you wonder why you were not invited to the wedding."

Ares felt the sting of his words as she says, "Our job here is done."

Atlas snaps his hands, and they disappear.

Violence turns around and walks inside as Athena and Wrath look at each other coming to a common understanding as they follow.

Violence gets inside as Heresy follows closely to his father as he says, "Father, what was the point of that?"

Violence responds, "Your sister's nature is discord. I'm not sure why she was here, but she is trying to rattle our teamwork." Violence turns around and sees Wrath and Athena in lock step as he says, "It might have worked."

Heresy turns and sees them, then he looks back to his father, concerned.

Violence looks at Heresy as he says, "Return and defend the humans. I will try to de-escalate the situation."

Heresy nods as he walks away as Athena approaches and says, "Brother, we must talk."

Wrath adds, "There is no reason to talk. You already know he is going to take the deal."

Violence looks at her, disgusted, as he responds, "Why would I take the deal?"

Wrath looks at him disgusted, as she says, "So that way you can be happy."

Violence looks at her confused as she punches him in the center mass as flames make an explosion, knocking him back.

She summons her armor, and so does Athena. Violence flies through a wall and finds himself in the cafeteria. He stands up and grunts as he prepares for what is to come.

Athena and Wrath walk through the hole on the wall that they made with Violence's body as they see the dust settle and Violence's bloodthirsty armor glowing through the dust.

Violence slams his spear in the ground and yells, "This is your last chance to stand down."

Wrath yells back, "No one will stand down to a self-made slave."

Violence pulls his spear out of the ground and moves to the battle as Wrath and Athena wait for him to get closer.

Heresy makes it to the control, and he sees them watching.

The doctor turns to Heresy and says, "What happened?"

Heresy takes a breath and says, "My sister is what happened." He scurries to the cameras as he sees the doctor documenting everything.

Heresy stares at the research as the doctor says, "Your guy's anatomy is beautiful but highly volatile."

Heresy moves his eyes back to the camera as Cerberus hides under Heresy. Heresy says under his breath, "You haven't seen volatile yet."

Aten looks at his controls as fire alarms, and troops are being deployed.

Heresy quickly says, "Call them off before they die."

Aten sternly says, "They are my soldiers, and they are equipped now."

Heresy pulls him to the camera as it shows Athena letting loose a thunderbolt, and it shreds a wall.

Heresy says, "These are three angels that are on par with the four horsemen. They will disintegrate everyone till they have reached their goal."

Aten says, "Fuck!" as he pushes the stand-down button.

Heresy says to him, "You just saved a lot of men."

Aten turns to the screen to see Violence tossing Wrath through a wall and seeing a bolt of lightning knocking Violence in a different direction in the cafeteria. He hears a yell that sounds like a thousand men.

Violence takes his spear and moves to Athena and Wrath. He gets close enough, and Athena thrust her spear at Violence. Violence dodges left, making the spear miss, while Wrath moves around Violence to move him into a crossfire. Violence senses it and donkey kicks her back, staggering her. Athena charges him, pushing him back, as Wrath lets loose a fire bolt, but it hits Violence's shield. Violence regains his footing and swing his spears at both of them, forcing them to take a step back from being hit by the spear tip. Violence spins the spear and places it on the front of shield, focusing on both of them, as his shield pulses, waiting for blood.

Wrath moves next to Athena as electricity flows from her fingertip. Athena lets loose a bolt from her hand as it strikes Violence's shield and pushes him back. Wrath chargers forward and jumps over Violence, letting a fire bolt go as it hit Violence's back where his armor does not cover. Violence grunts in pain as his skin sears shut. Violence charges at Athena's shield, bashing her through the nearest wall. As he throws her off his shield, he quickly turns and throws his spear at Wrath, skimming her shoulder, making her bleed a little.

Violence summons his kopis and says, "I do not want this."

Athena shoots a bolt from other side of the wall. As it strikes his back, Wrath charges him and grabs his neck in a choke hold as Athena charges at Violence. Violence doesn't flinch with Wrath being on his back as she waits for Athena to get closer as she thrust her sword at Violence. Violence parries her sword and kicks her back as Wrath squeezes with all her might, trying to get Violence to budge.

Violence whispers, "We have done kinkier than this, love."

Wrath, hearing this, make her even more aggravated as she digs her nails in his throat.

He chuckles as he says, "Well, that's new." He jumps up and lands on Wrath, as she gasps from the weight that just landed on her. He takes her foot and throws her into another room as Athena hits him with a thunderbolt, sending him reeling back.

Violence feels that one as he yells, "Hoo!"

It sounds like ten thousands Spartans as it echoes through the facility.

Athena charges through as Violence catches her midair, and he slams her down with a crimson blast. She goes through a table, and a sound of her human body cracking is heard. He places his foot on her chest and begins to press down. Wrath lets loose a wave of flames, which pushes both of them back. Violence armor is smoldering from the heat. As it begins to melt, he looks at it and rips off his armor and throws the hot-as-hell metal chest plate at Athena. As it hits the ground, it scatters into fragments, leaving a piece in Athena. She groans, still trying to get up from the slam from Violence.

Violence turns his attention to Wrath as she stands and yells, "Is this what you are? Look what you have done."

Violence responds, "This is what I am forced to do due to your actions."

Wrath lets go of another flame wave, and it pushes Violence back into a wall, pinning him, as she continues to hold the wave. He feels the heat scorching his skin. He gets enough strength and slams his back into the wall, making the wall cave in. Wrath holds the wave as she is on the run. She looks to Athena for help, but her unconscious body has taken too much damage and needs a rest. She presses forward knowing that she is on her own.

Heresy and the others sit in the control room as they watch the event unfold. They look, and Aten moves to another computer and can see all the alarms going off, ushering for him to take precautions. Heresy can see the urgency on Aten's face as he walks over and sees all the alarms begging to go in effect.

Heresy looks at the cameras and sees Violence and Wrath standing in a hallway as he thinks, *Now is the time.* Heresy says, "What precautions does this plan have?"

Aten responds, "The fire extinguishers for one."

Heresy responds, "Be serious, please."

Aten retorts aggressively, "I am being serious."

The doctor chimes in quickly, "Blast door, tasers—honestly, the works. Anything in particular you are looking for?"

Heresy thinks and says, "Close the cafeteria."

Aten presses a sequence of buttons as he shut the blast-proof door to the cafeteria, leaving Athena in the room alone as she sleeps.

Aten says, "Now what?"

Heresy responds, "Wait for them to enter one of the rooms and then seal it shut. They will either kill each other or talk it out."

The doctor responds quickly, "So just like humans?"

Heresy responds to the question, "My father and mother are more like humans than they will ever admit."

Violence and Wrath look around, seeing bunker-level security walls shut around them.

Wrath turns to him and asks, "Is this your doing?"

Violence looks at her, unshaken, then responds sarcastically, "Yes, this is my doing."

Wrath gets annoyed by Violence not being helpful. Heat radiates off her, causing a heat wave. Violence body starts to char from the heat. He takes a knee from the pain as he grunts. Wrath can see the pain she is inflicting and summons her spear. As she continues pulsing the wave, she walks to him as he is can't move and stabs Violence in the shoulder. He winces in pain as his angelic armor begins to cover his body, shining a white light.

Wrath gets annoyed as she mutters, "You are no longer worthy of that armor," as she digs the spear in deeper. The armor reaches the spear and begins to dig it out of Violence. Wrath pushes deeper as her skin begins to tear from the energy she is expending. Violence grasp the spear as he begins to push it out, and his skin begins to tear as well. Violence pushes the spear out of his body, and the armor fully forms. Wrath begins to lose her control as she pushes farther as her skin starts to burst. Violence pulls his dagger off his chest and slices her thigh. As she releases her wave, he quickly moves, grabbing the spear. She grabs it with both hands to try to stay in control. He pushes her on the wall and presses the spear on the wall, pinning her to the wall.

Wrath spits on Violence, then says, "You are nothing but an animal."

Violence looks at her annoyed and disgusted as he yells at her, "I am your animal!"

Wrath sees the emotions in his eyes as she shuts up.

Violence continues, "Do you think there wasn't a day I did not think about you?"

Wrath thinks back to the time that she could almost feel Violence standing behind her in hell.

Violence continues his verbal assault. "What do you think is my biggest regret? Fuck it, I'm not waiting for an answer. Me leaving you was my regret."

Wrath sees the truth in her eyes as she starts to relax and feel regret. Violence drops his knife and places it on the cut of her thigh as he begins to heal her. She feels his warm hand as she feels the cut, and her burns start to disappear. Violence can feel her yearning to be let go as she tries to move her hands. He pushes her hand back and looks at her eyes. Her eyes meet his as they return to their angelic colors.

He says, "Not so fast there, wife." Wrath smiles as he commands her as he continues, "I like seeing you like this. Let me enjoy it for a minute."

Wrath giggles as she says, "You like seeing me pinned?"

Violence moves his head closer to her as she leans in for a kiss. He teases her more by not giving in right away. She makes a pouting noise as he smiles at her anticipation.

He finally whispers, "I like it when I am the one pinning you." He kisses her gently as she smiles. He finally releases her as her hands go over his wounds as they kiss into the night.

18

A tlas and the others reach the cave. He sits down as the others are celebrating a false victory. Atlas studies their behavior, and he sees everything is normal except for Ares. She seems standoffish as she is with the group, but she is playing a part. He sees her smile fade as her true face comes out, and it seems she is worried. He gets up and walks to her slowly as not to alarm her. She turns around and sees him towering over her. The group looks at them, and they can sense something is about to happen as they watch Atlas grabs Ares forcefully. She looks back at the group to see their reaction as he spins her head around.

He stares in her eyes as he says, "How many half-truths have you told me?" Atlas's hand begins to have a shadow form around it as her essence is being drained.

She smiles and confidently says, "More than enough." Her form disappears into a shadow as she disappears.

The group looks at the shadow as Gluttony says, "She was never even here to begin with."

Atlas smiles as he holds his hand up, still restraining a shadow. He studies it as and finds out where she is. He also sees the last watcher has been hiding with her this whole time. He studies it more, then smiles knowing they are in the Middle East.

—⚍—

Violence wakes up before Wrath. He gets up to wake up Wrath. He looks at her stretch, watching her as she wakes up.

He smiles at her and says, "Good morning, love."

She says groggily, "Good morning, love." She smiles and gets up to kiss Violence.

He smiles as he breaks the kiss, and they get dressed.

Wrath looks at the blast doors still confining them. Wrath touches the door, and it is ice cold. Violence punches a hole open to let them out.

Wrath looks at Violence as she asks, "Why must everything you do always be overkill?"

Violence grabs her waist and pulls her closer, then says, "That is one of things that you love about me."

Wrath kisses him on the cheek, smiles,and moves away from him as they exit their cell.

As they walk out, the alarms go off again. Violence groans, annoyed by the sound as they move to the control room. They pass the cafeteria, and Violence looks to see where he left his sister, but she is not there anymore. They reach the room and see it closed off. Violence goes to break again, but Wrath steps in his path and looks at him and says, "Watch and learn." She turns and knocks on the door. There is a slight pause, and Violence looks at her. She looks back as she holds a pausing finger up.

The blast doors open as they see everyone in there. Heresy is pulling the infernal metal out of Athena's back. She groans as the metal leaves her skin. He throws the metal on the ground, and it disintegrates into nothing.

Athena sees them, and she says, "I must admit, brother, your armor becoming a grenade is clever."

Violence walks over to her and says, "We have much to talk about, sister, but now is not the time. So I offer an olive branch."

Wrath follows him and nods to Athena that she is also on the same side.

Violence holds his hand out as she thinks and grabs Violence forearm and they shake on it as she says, "Truce then."

Violence smiles as he says, "At least of now."

Athena smiles as she says, "At least for now." Heresy pulls another piece out. She groans while saying, "I tracked your daughter to a place in Mesopotamia. It appear to be in a cave."

Wrath and Violence look at the tracker as they look shocked.

Athena sees their faces as she asks, "What is it?"

Violence smiles as he looks Wrath, and he says, "That is where we would meet. Who knew our daughter would be so sentimental."

—⁓—

Atlas teleports his team to a temple in Mesopotamia and approaches a giant stone doorway.

Limbo looks at the doorway made of stone and asks snuggly, "Why would humans make a doorway so large when they are so tiny."

Atlas responds to question quietly, "It is because this wasn't built by humans. It was built by giants. Some of them I called my own kin."

Gluttony looks at Atlas and begins to read Atlas, seeing Atlas go through memory lane as he looks around. Gluttony ask curiously, "What does this place mean to you?"

Atlas responds quietly, "It is where I was taken prisoner by a false god." Atlas snaps out of his vulnerable state as he signals them to move in by nodding his head.

Atlas walks in first, and the group follows closely. They start to hear quiet voices around them. Limbo and Gluttony begins to feel like someone is gripping the insides of their stomach, like an overload of anxiety as they keep pressing forward.

Limbo begins to hear the voices, becoming clearer as he stops to listen.

The voice says, "The middle child even to this day, you still can't find any respect or belonging."

Limbo stops and looks around as he wonders where the voices are coming from.

The voices continue saying, "No love of any kind. I have never seen such a sad angel. It must be hard to go on day in and day out just floating into oblivion."

Limbo feels the truth in the words as his eyes start to swell up. Gluttony looks at him and sees the despair and shame in his eyes. Gluttony tries to keep up with Atlas.

The voices continue to badger Limbo relentlessly.

"Even your own group would rather leave you here. Why can you not be like your brother Ares?"

Limbo collapses on the ground as the voices continue to terrorize Limbo. He is paralyzed.

Gluttony tries his best to keep up with Atlas as he hears the voices start to come in clearer.

"Demeter, I cannot believe you are not gorging yourself like your father with children."

Demeter looks around, and she sees where her uncle is walking toward.

The voices continue. "I wonder how your daughter is doing right now. Do you think she would even approve of this?"

Demeter thinks about Persephone and all the havoc she caused, unaware that her daughter was given away without her knowledge. Demeter's throat begins to swell as the voices continue.

"I found it quite poetic when you were wrathful. How many mothers had to watch their son and daughter shrivel away due to your famine?"

Demeter slows down as she remembers seeing young children dead and malnourished, their mothers and father starving themselves, looking unto their children with guilt in their eyes.

The voice continues speaking. "How many humans followed your kind's path, turning to and devouring whatever part of their children that still have substance." The voice giggles as it says, "You reap what you sow...how fitting it is right now."

Demeter falls and begins to shake uncontrollably as her thought overwhelms here senses, and she begins to have a seizure.

Atlas turns around to keep track of his team and sees them all on the ground. He says, annoyed, as he heads back to pick them up, "You are so weak. Words are the thing that leaves you in a state of disarray." Atlas picks up Gluttony and then turns to Demeter and picks her up as he says, "You are not deserving of the title Titan, my dear niece."

Atlas gets closer as he begins to feel the same feeling as the voice come to badger him now.

"Atlas, the most untested Titan of them all. Born too early to help, born too late to do anything about it."

Atlas continues to move as the voices continue, "There is no path where you prove yourself... young one."

Atlas continues to move unfazed as he says to no one but the dark cave that he traversing.

"I spent what felt like an eternity with only myself and my thoughts. This is not a battle you will win."

The voice continues as it says, "If you think that was eternity, just wait to you see what eternity really is."

Atlas smiles as he says, "You are about to find out, Ares." Before he could react, he feels a knife puncture his middle thigh. He jolts at the pain, pulling his leg back and taking the user with it. He looks at the shadow eyes as he says, "Clever, truly your father's daughter."

Atlas moves closer as he reaches a small room lit with sunlight. There is a small exit on the roof. Atlas moves to the center as he drops his team. He sees two more shadows come out, taking the form of Demeter, Boreas, and Ares. Atlas waits and summons his sword as he hears wings flapping. He focuses on the sound and its trajectory. He turns and throws his sword, striking the angel in the back and stapling him to cave's wall. Ares true form comes out in shock as she sees the angel's blood pouring out like a waterfall.

Atlas looks at Ares as he says, "Now it's your turn, traitor."

The shadows begin to form around him like a wolf pack, trying to take a lesson out of her father's book. Atlas sees the tactic as he smiles and pushes forward to Limbo's shadow, catching them off guard and slams the shadow to the ground as it the shadow shatters falling, back into the darkness. The other two regroup as Ares pulls her swords. One of them is a katana bleeding a shadow around it, and the other is a wakizashi. Atlas stands his ground, waiting for their first move. Ares starts to think. Ares charges at Atlas. Atlas tries to counter her by punching to where he expects her to be. She jumps over him as the other shadow gets on his back and puts him in a choke hold. Atlas begins to get annoyed as he slams the shadow in the nearest wall. The shadow breaks as Atlas makes himself stagger by hitting the wall too hard. Ares is following as she tries to impale him her two weapons. Atlas grabs the blades as they are going toward him and catches them on the dull side. Ares pushes harder as Atlas stops her and headbutts her as she staggers back. He rips the wakizashi out her hand and stabs her neck and kicks her in the dirt as she bleeds out and gargles out the word, "Father," as her body turns into a mask. He reaches down and takes the mask as the others start to recover, no longer hearing the voices.

Atlas looks at them disappointed as they look down in shame.

He starts, "How do you let word defeat you? Are you really that weak? You are undeserving of the title Titan." Atlas punches a wall of frustration and yells in the cave.

The other shudder to his war cry as they stand in silence.

Atlas takes a deep breath and calmly says, "We need to be better. Training your mind is just as important as the body."

He looks up at the dead angel hanging on the wall. He begins to climb the wall and pulls his sword out as the body hit the floor with a thud. Atlas hops down and retrieve the horn of the corps as it the body turns to ash. Atlas looks at the silver horn, and a bright light shines down, and Saint Michael appears. He steps forward, then says, "So what is the next step from here?"

Atlas picks up the mask, then says, "We free my kin."

Saint Michael nods his head and stares in to Atlas's eyes as he nods.

19

res is in the gym when he feels a crushing feeling in his stomach and hears a faint, "Father." He looks around and goes to leave the gym and finds Wrath. He sees her looking at him in the hallway with her eyes red and puffy. Violence runs over to her and holds her as she starts sobbing in Violence's chest.

Athena turns the corner and sees the pain in what is happening. Violence looks up and motions her away. Athena walks away as she fears the worse to see Wrath in that state.

Wrath says through her sob, "Ares is gone."

Violence holds her tighter and says, "He will suffer."

Heresy walks up behind them, and Wrath feels his presence. She reaches her hand behind her. Heresy sees the hand and takes it as he gets pulled in to his mother's arms.

Wrath says through the sobbing, "Do not leave our side ever." She pulls his face to her eyes as she shakes him while saying, "Do you understand?"

Heresy holds his mother, making him feel like a child again, as he grabs his mother tighter and says, "Yes, Mother."

Violence says in a low tone, "We have to get to the stone hedge. That is the only gateway for Cronus to get out of his level of hell."

Wrath lets go of her baby as she looks at Violence and nods, determined. They march into the control room, and they see Athena talking to Aten.

Violence interrupts them, saying, "We need a lift to the stone hedge."

Aten looks up and sees the pain and anguish in their eyes. He picks up a radio and says, "Attention, pilots, wheels up in ten. Sending coordinates now."

Violence and the group walk to the hanger as a pilot directs them to an Osprey.

—∞—

Atlas and the group portal to the stone hedge, and he looks at the stones sticking out the ground. He walks over to it and examines it. He touches one, and it starts to hum to life and shows runes of old magic.

Saint Michael looks over his shoulder and says, "What are those?"

Atlas rubs his fingers on it as he says, "It is our old language." He sighs and continues, "It says, 'Here lies the baby eater.'" Atlas walks over to the next one. He touches it, and it hums to life.

Saint Michael walks over to another and touches it, and nothing happens.

Saint Michael says, "Why does it not hum when I touch it?"

Atlas responds, "For the same reason why you are here. You are no Titan yet."

Atlas continues as he places his hand on the stone. A sharp stones poke his skin, breaking it, and he bleeds on the stone. The other stones turn on as it creates a hole for an offering. Atlas pulls Ares's mask and places it in one of them. The hole begins to develop a green flame inside.

Atlas looks at the others and is about to say something but is cut off when he sees an Osprey flying overhead.

Saint Michael eyes become fixed as his wings begin to flutter.

Atlas looks at Saint Michael and sternly says, "We do the mission first."

Saint Michael nods as he places his hand in one of the stones, and a flame develops around his hand. He gets a shiver as he feels power, hunger, and coldness. The others follow suit. The stones start to glow green as a heptagon starts to glow green on the ground.

Alas looks around as a rocket hits his shoulder, doing just annoyance damage. He turns around and sees Violence and everyone standing on a hill behind them as the Osprey flies away.

Saint Michael yells, "Now what?"

Atlas takes his hand out and motions everyone to him, then he says, "It will take time. He is waking up from a deep coma." He looks over to Saint Michael, who is staring at the man brandishing a spear on the hill. Saint Michael looks at Atlas and demands, "Give me one of the horns."

Atlas looks at him confused and says, "Why?"

Saint Michael continues, "Just in case you try to betray me."

Atlas looks irritated as he says, "Now is not the time for distrust."

Saint Michael quickly retorts, "Exactly. Now hand over one of the horns."

Atlas looks even more annoyed but hands it over with a warning, "You are being reckless."

Saint Michael stares at him and says, "I am the better warrior, Atlas."

Atlas looks annoyed and goes back to the stone hedge and watches it hum more and more to life.

—⟋⟍⟍—

Violence and the groups see the stone hedges getting activated, and Athena says, "We do not have much time left."

Violence yells at the pilot, "Take us down on the hill!"

The Osprey land behind a hill, and they get out.

Violence yells behind him to the pilot, "Does this thing have any power?"

The copilot yells back, "We have hell missiles."

Violence looks confused as he yells back, "Hit the big one with one and then get clear."

The pilot yells back, "Roger that, sir."

The Osprey lifts off when the group is cleared and watches the group climb the hill as the pilot lets loose a missile at Atlas. The Osprey sees the Titan tank the missile to no damage and quickly changes directions, then flies away.

Violence looks down and sees his brother with Atlas. He turns to Athena and can see the shock on her face. Violence summons his hell armor and spear. He can feel Saint Michael burning a hole in the helmet as the both stare each other down.

Violence looks at Atlas, and he can see him planning. Violence turns to Athena slowly and says, "What do you propose, sister?"

Athena sighs as she says, "I think diplomacy is out of the question. Heresy, blow the horn."

Heresy turns to her and says, "We do not have the other ones."

Athena responds, "As long as they are blown, they will alert the other angels."

Heresy takes the horn and blows it loud as the clear sky begins to develop overcast.

Violence smiles as Athena stares at him and says, "What is funny, brother?"

Violence's eyes glow red crimson, and he responds, "We shall fight in the shade."

Athena rolls her eyes as she says, "We have to be smart, brother."

Violence responds to her jab with his own, "Shall we ask the owl about this?"

Athena rolls her eyes.

Wrath grabs Violence's attention, then says with caution, "Husband, do not kill your brother."

Violence responds to her, "I will not provoke him, but I feel my hands being tied more and more."

Wrath responds, "Just try, my love."

Violence reaches and grabs her hand and turns to her then says, "I do not want to kill my brother. I just...I do not want to."

Wrath can see the pain in his eyes and can see the truth of his words that he just spoke. Violence looks down and begins walking down the hill to meet them.

—⚋—

Atlas sees their movement as he flies and pulls up the rest of the soldier he has left. Four hellish soldiers and two scorpions pop up out the ground as they await orders. Atlas gives the command to move forward as the scorpions take off under the dirt and the soldiers head off toward them.

Saint Michael sees Atlas's command as he says commandingly, "Ares is mine."

Atlas looks back as he says, "They will not kill him, just isolating him." Atlas looks at Limbo and motions him to come to him.

Limbo sees the command as he sheepishly walks away.

Atlas waits for him to get closer and says, "Your brother has chosen to thin the bloodline. Put a dome among them when they are alone."

Limbo looks at Atlas and says, "They will just break through it."

Atlas smiles at Limbo, giving Limbo a chill up his spine. Atlas continues, "Blood ice."

Limbo looks at him in shock. Limbo looks to Saint Michael, and Saint Michael nods to him in agreement. Then Limbo looks at Atlas as Atlas says, "This is what war looks likes, my young Titan." Limbo nods, understanding his role.

Saint Michael sees an opportunity as the group is making quick work on the soldiers. He sees Ares isolated. Limbo sees the movement as he starts to flex and grunt as the spell is being conjured. When Saint Michael reaches Ares, he summons the blood ice dome on them, trapping them inside with a clear view. Limbo passes out from the spell.

Atlas looks at Gluttony, then says, "Take him far away from here. My father might not be so kind on seeing angels on his arrival." Atlas summons a portal as Gluttony takes him away through the portal.

Violence and the group are making quick work out of the soldiers as they slowly press Violence away from the group. Violence cuts a soldier in half and feels another presence when he is kicked by Saint Michael, pushing him far enough away from the group. Saint Michael closes the gap, then blood ice starts to form around them, making an arena.

Wrath sees what's happing as she shoots a fire bolt through a soldier, killing it. She runs over the dome and begins to try to melt it but to no avail. Heresy and Athena see the dome, and they head over as well.

Athena looks to the stone hedge and sees Gluttony and Limbo escape. She sees Atlas waiting by the stone hedge, and she thinks, *Clever.*

Violence gets up and sees his brother's sword drawn but allowing him to get up.

Saint Michael looks at his brother, then says, "Your time has come, brother. It is time of them to see that I am the superior angel of war."

Violence stands up, looking at him as he responds, "You do not want this responsibility, brother."

Saint Michael stays glaring at Violence as he retorts, "All your teasing, all your followers, and all your glory will be mine."

Violence looks confused as he responds curiously, "What glory?"

Saint Michael looks even more annoyed and says, "Even after all the changes, people still worship you. They still say your name even though I am the superior version of you."

Violence laughs as he responds, "You are no a superior version or anything like me."

Saint Michael gets annoyed by that answer as his wings flutters and he charges at Violence.

Violence sees Saint Michael's wings flutter. As he anticipates the charge, he dodges left, and Saint Michael swings his sword back but is parried by Violence's shield. Saint Michael stagger back and quickly turns around, assuming Violence would chase him down. Saint Michael sees Violence just standing there with a look of guilt on his face. Violence thinks about the time he was watching him grow up, wanting to spar with Ares as he shoos him off.

Violence thinks, *Would things be different if I just spent more time with him?*

Saint Michael gets more annoyed as he presses Violence. Violence doesn't move. Saint Michael slashes his sword downward as Violence doesn't move and cuts his breastplate. Violence comes back to reality and moves to a defensive position. Violence presses Saint Michael and his shield bashes him back, making Saint Michael stand up quickly as he sees Violence taking his breastplate off. Saint Michael takes advantage of him taking his armor off as he charges at him. Violence throws his chest piece at Saint Michael. Saint Michael takes off in to the air and dives down at Violence, missing with his sword but knocking him to the ice wall. Saint Michael flies off as Violence looks behind him and sees Wrath behind the ice staring at him, concerned for him. Saint Michael turns and sees them having a moment, maligning him. He erupts in jealousy. Saint Michael shines a beam of light down on Violence, blinding him. Violence curls up in a defensive position, blinded by the light. Violence puts his hand on the ground, and he sees Saint Michael charging him. Violence lunges and meets him, catching him off guard, digging his shield in the chest of Saint Michael. Saint Michael loses his focus as the beam of light disappears.

Violence shrugs Saint Michael off and says, "We do not have to do this, brother."

Saint Michael snarls back, "You will know my glory."

Saint Michael takes off the air and starts flying around. Violence tries to keep up with him, but the helmet is constricting. Saint Michael sees an opening and dives down, slicing Violence's leg and then taking off to the air again. Violence growls as he takes his helmet off and slams his sword in the ground and pulls his chain out. Saint Michael smiles and flies around again as Violence starts to swing his chain in an *x* formation. Saint Michael sees another opening and dives down again. Violence moves and slams the chain, catching his wings. Saint Michael hits the ground hard and tries to get up, but Violence has wrapped his chain around his wing. Violence begins to reel him in as Saint Michael tries to get away. It is too late as he feels Violence's kopis piercing his wing into the ground. Saint Michael yells in pain as he tries to get away. Violence, with his eyes burning crimson, takes his other wing and begins to tear it off. The sound of tearing skin, cartilage tearing, and the painful screams fill the dome. Violence lets go of Saint Michael as he tries to crawl away. He flips over and looks at Violence with disbelief.

Saint Michael stands up and says, "You are only an animal."

Violence responds, "You are forcing my hand here out of your own greed."

Saint Michael screams, "I am the future. You are the past!"

Violence walks over to him and punches him in the chest, leaving a crimson blast as he hits the ground again. Saint Michael grunts as Violence bends down to him and says, "Do you yield, brother?"

Saint Michael, chocking on his own word, manages to get out, "Would you?"

Violence begins to choke on his words too. "You are no brother."

Saint Michael tries to throw another punch at Violence, but he is too weak. Violence looks down and grabs his chain and wraps it around his neck. Violence grabs Saint Michael's sword and jumps and slams it into the ice as he throws the chain around the sword. He walks back over to his brother and looks into his eyes. Violence sees that Saint Michael's eyes are no longer a light color but full of dark swirls.

Violence holds his brother as he says, "I am proud of you, brother. I am sorry, but I will be here for you in the end."

Saint Michael closes his eyes and begins to tear up as he says, "Fuck you, Ares."

Violence grabs the chain and lifts him up, chocking him. Violence holds the chain with one hand and with the other hand holds his brother's hand till he feels his life leave his body. Violence lets go as the blood ice melts almost instantly.

Wrath runs to Violence as she looks at Violence holding his dead brother's hand as his body lies on the ground lifeless. Violence looks up at Wrath, not able to say a word. Wrath looks at him and just hugs him as he tries to speak but can't.

Wrath whispers calmly, "You did what you had to."

Athena stays silent, unsure about what to say.

Violence lets go of his dead brother's hand as he stands up clears his throat. "We still have a job to do."

Athena watches her brother's resilience as he looks at Atlas waiting for them.

Violence summons his angelic armor ready for the battle to come. He takes one last look at his brother and says, "I wish you were better, brother. Maybe I wouldn't have to live with this guilt now."

Wrath stands in silence. Heresy pats his dad's back, motivated by his father's focus. Violence looks at his son and nods his head, showing strength.

20

tlas watches Violence walk away victorious. He looks
disappointed but not shocked at the result. Violence and Atlas
stare each other down from a distance as Violence and the
others begin to move down to him. Atlas pulls his sword out and slams
it in the ground and waits for them. He watches how they walk, reading
them as they walk to him. He watches how they move. He realizes
Heresy and Wrath are walking unsure. He pays attention to Athena
and sees her walking to him like she is going to her everyday job. He
shifts his attention to Violence and sees how he is walking confidently
toward him. He smiles and looks behind him to see the ritual is starting
to work as the ground starts to crack. He hears the next horn go off as
the sun begins to eclipse.

He thinks, *Arrogant angel.*

They begin to get closer, and he pulls his sword out of the ground.

Violence stops, signaling everyone else to hold for a moment.

Athena stops and says, "What is it, brother? We are running out
of time."

Violence turns to her, saying, "Is there an easier way to do this?"

Athena replies, "Probably not."

Violence looks around says, "What if we break the stones?"

Athena thinks for a bit and says, "I do not believe that would work,
brother. That sounds too simple."

Violence looks at Wrath, then says, "Want to help me break a
stone?"

Heresy chimes in, "Me and Athena can hold Atlas to give it a shot."

Wrath looks at Heresy as she says, "You be safe. I will not lose another child today."

Heresy hugs his mom and whispers, "We do it for her."

Wrath eyes start to tear up, and she hears Violence says, "If anyone is going to die here today, make sure I am first."

Wrath snaps around and says, "No more of us die today. You hear me."

Violence smiles as he says, "I love you, Aphrodite."

Wrath's eyes begin to glow rainbow again as she lets go of Heresy and hugs Violence.

Wrath says quietly, "No more death for us."

Violence holds her tighter as he says, "I will try to avoid the glory then."

Wrath looks up at Violence and kisses him before they begin to move in.

Atlas watches it all unfold as he stays silent for their moment, hoping it would distract them a while longer as the ground hums more. They finally reach similar ground where they can hear each other casually.

Atlas starts the conversation.

"There is still time for all of you to join me."

Athena retorts quickly, "Not a chance in hell, Atlas. You have forced our hand."

Violence stares him down.

Atlas takes a deep breath, then says, "Good. You are all not worthy of our Titanhood anyways."

Athena quickly jumps and attempts to slam her spear down on Atlas. Atlas sidesteps it quickly as he read Heresy's attack and parries it. Violence moves behind him and slashes his long sword at his back. Atlas luckily moves out of its way, dodging Violence's attack. Atlas swings his sword horizontally, making space as he recovers from the quick burst of everyone's attack. Violence and Wrath sneak off as Atlas is distracted by Athena and Heresy.

Violence and Wrath look at the stone as Wrath begins to study the words.

Violence looks at her as he says, "I keep on forgetting you are a part of the Titan family."

Wrath continues to read as she says, "I am a part of our family." Wrath keeps studying it as she says, "There is nothing we can do."

Violence looks at Wrath and says shocked, "What do you mean?"

Wrath slowly back up as she says, "There is nothing we can do. This was built during the Titan age."

Violence looks annoyed as she continues, "This was blessed by Cronus himself as a resurrection tool."

Violence looks at the battle as Athena is thrown away and Heresy tries his hardest to hold him off till she gets back. Wrath sees the struggle, and because her fear of losing another child, she quickly rushes to him.

Violence takes one more looks at the stone and has a thought. He takes his longsword and slashes it. He looks at it as nothing happens as he mumbles, "I do not know what to expect out of that." Violence turns around as he hears a wounding groan and sees Atlas has jammed Heresy's trident into his upper thigh. Atlas turns around and kicks Athena, knocking her unconscious. Violence watches Wrath try to let a blaze hit Atlas. Atlas undercuts it barely as he charges at her and tackles her to the ground and is about to begin a vicious ground and pound. Atlas raises a fist that is quickly caught with Violence's chain. Wrath looks up at Atlas. Atlas looks at his hand, then punches powerfully at Wrath, making her dazed, unable move. Atlas looks at her in a domineering way. "You will make an excellent slave wife."

Atlas feels the jerk of the chain pull him slightly.

Violence jerks the chain again as crimson burst yanks Atlas off Wrath, and with one fell swoop, Atlas jerks the chain as he did in the Aztec temple, sending Violence flying toward him ready to catch Violence in his grip. Violence readies himself as he flies toward Atlas, sending his feet first into his chest, which sends him stumbling back.

Atlas looks confused, getting caught in his own arrogance. "So you do learn."

Violence lets the chain go and summons his longsword, staying silent.

Atlas calls for his sword out of the ground by Wrath as it flies to his hand. Atlas looks at the green marks and sees more lines have disappeared.

Violence can feel his gaze shift and charges him. Atlas swings his sword up and is parried by Violence. As Violence's shield bashes him with a crimson burst, Atlas is sent reeling. Violence swings his sword, barely nicking his calf. Atlas looks at his leg, getting annoyed, as he charges Violence this time. Violence ducks and slides to left but is met with Atlas's fist, sending Violence rolling on the ground. Violence recovers quickly as he stands up and takes a defensive position. Atlas looks at him and charges again. This time Violence charges back, making the shield block the sword as a crimson burst follows, knocking his sword out of his hand. Violence clings to Atlas and attempts to stab him. Atlas catches Violence's thrust and squeezes his hand, making Violence release his sword and shield. Violence lets a left hook fly as it meets Atlas's chin, letting loose a crimson burst. Atlas releases Violence, astonished by the blow, as he holds his chin. Atlas, dazed, can sense Violence's stare; and he begins to feel a shiver down his back. Violence takes a deep breath and can begin to smell a caramel aroma. Violence begins to rushes him, getting close, as Atlas swings down, determined to knock Violence into the ground. Violence blocks it but makes him kneel from the power behind the punch. Atlas presses down harder and sees Violence's eyes glowing a full crimson red. Violence swiftly stands up as a crimson burst flows beneath him. Violence successfully closes the gap and lays a solid punch in his ribcage, releasing a crimson blast. Atlas shudders at the blow, and Violence rips the horns away and throws them as close as he can to the other angels.

Atlas feels the horns come loose, and his urgency was brutal as he leads an onslaught of fury on Violence. Violence tanks and dodges to the best of his ability, but eventually, the Titan's strength is too much to bear. Atlas's hands grabs Violence by the chest as he begins to squeeze hard, making Violence's eyes bleed crimson. Violence looks down as Atlas picks him up and takes off his helmet and slams it in Atlas's face. The three spikes dig into the Titan's face as he releases and rips it out, angered, but is met with Violence's onslaught of brutal blows. Atlas tries his best to recover as Violence lands blow after blow. Atlas swings wildly, trying to get Violence under control. Eventually, Atlas lands one in Violence's sternum. Violence staggers backward, and Atlas closes the gap as he grab Violence by the neck. Violence musters the last of his strength and spits in Atlas's face and says, "Titan scum."

Atlas looks at Violence and wipes the spit off, responding, "Not many angels could do what you just did. What shall be your final name?"

Wrath and Athena regain consciousness to see Violence in dire need, but they don't have the strength to help him.

Violence looks at Atlas and says, "The Gardner."

Atlas looks confused as he has heard that name before, then he hears a knife being pulled from Violence. Atlas closes his grip, completely making Violence dissipate into ash. As the mask falls, his wedding ring falls as well.

Heresy's and Athena see the horns and begin crawling toward them as Wrath, in rage, lets loose flame and embers at Atlas, letting her raw emotions dictate her power. Atlas takes blow after blows as he is pushed back enough to where Wrath reaches the mask and ring. Atlas grabs the dagger and throws it at the mask, making it shudder and fall into pieces in her hands. Wrath looks up at Atlas, the pain in her eyes could kill even a Titan at this point. Atlas sees her eyes glowing a dark fiery red, and he says, "Now you know my pain, slave."

She grabs the ring as the crimson begins to swirl around her finger, mixing with her flame. Atlas looks at the ritual and can see a figure's horns glowing. A dark emerald green starts to come up. They hear an ungodly groan as Cronus begins to rise, speaking old Titan language as he sighs in victory. She holds her hands up and lets loose a burning crimson on him. Atlas begins to melt away as he hears the horns being blown, and a searing bright light beams on the stone hedge. Cronus looks at the direction the sound being made and lets a ray of emerald green hit Heresy. He begins to shudder and scream in the light as Wrath holds the blaze, and her skin starts to tear apart as the screams of Atlas starts to dissipate with his body. Heresy falls back into the mask form, fueling Wrath even more with passion, making the flame turn blue as the Titan turns to nothing but a skeleton. She continues to burn to skeleton out of rage as Cronus turns into ash as well. Wrath continues until she passes out from the energy she used.

Heresy and Athena limps over to Wrath, attempting to awake her but to no avail. A bright light shines down as Saint Peter walks out of it and looks at the battle that has just happened. Athena sees Saint Peter, and out of respect, she barely stands up.

Saint Peter nods his heads to acknowledge it and walks over to Wrath while saying, "Rest now, child, you have done more than enough. Out of all the timelines we can see this victory was the least probable."

Saint Peter bends over to Wrath and places his hand on her forehead as she slowly wakes up. Saint Peter watches her. "Be calm now, child. I can sense the anguish."

Wrath looks around as she is hoping it was just a nightmare. She feels her hand and can feel his ring. She looks at the ring and starts to break down in tears.

Saint Peter walks over to Heresy and pulls the trident out as Heresy groans in pain. Saint Peter places his hand on the wound and heals it. Heresy moves to his mother to comfort her as Saint Peter walks back to his center. Wrath, Heresy, and Athena stand and mourn Ares's death. Saint Peter begins to chuckle.

Wrath snaps at him, "One of heavens greatest warriors died today, a lot of angel died today. Show some respect."

Athena looks in shock and says, "I agree with Aphrodite."

Saint Peter holds his hands up to explain. "How curious though, for eons Ares was the bane of many existence, and now that he is gone. We see the true side of everybody."

Athena looks at Saint Peter in disbelief. "He is my brother regardless of his faults."

Saint Peter raises his hand and continues, "How far would you go to bring him back?"

Wrath looks at him with suspicion. "What do you mean?"

Saint Peter points to her hand. "Where was that created?"

Wrath looks at the black and red ring, trying to remember where he had them made. Wrath finally remembers at she looks up at Saint Peter. "Valhalla?"

Saint Peter nods. "He was a very clever angel. His mask was not true point where lives just how to summon his soul."

Wrath gets up and begins to think and how to get down there.

Athena looks at Saint Peter. "How do we get down there?"

Saint Peter smiles and says, "You will need these back." He waves his hands, and all of their wings pop out instantly.

Aphrodite looks at her rainbow-colored wings, almost unrecognizable to her now. Athena examines her silver wings and then looks back at Saint Peter.

Saint Peter sees the look in her eyes and says, "You will also be needing this to get him back. Try not to spend it all at once." He tosses a satchel full of coins at them as Aphrodite picks it up.

Heresy walks to his mother. "I will come with you. Let's go get Father."

Athena stands next to them as Saint Peter says, "Phobos, you are being tasked with your own mission. Find the traitors."

Phobos flutters his black wing with rainbow tips.

Saint Peter looks at Aphrodite and Athena, then says, "Good luck," and waves a portal to the underworld.